BLOOD PASSION
BOOK V
RACHAEL's REVENGE

J.M. VALENTE

Cover design by J. M. Valente

ReadersMagnet, LLC

Blood Passion: Book V - Rachael's Revenge
Copyright © 2022 by *JM Valente*

Published in the United States of America
ISBN   Paperback: 978-1-958030-19-6
ISBN   Hardback: 978-1-958030-25-7
ISBN   eBook: 978-1-958030-20-2

All rights reserved. No part of this publication may be reproduced, stored in a retrieval system or transmitted in any way by any means, electronic, mechanical, photocopy, recording or otherwise without the prior permission of the author except as provided by USA copyright law.

The opinions expressed by the author are not necessarily those of ReadersMagnet, LLC.

ReadersMagnet, LLC
10620 Treena Street, Suite 230 | San Diego, California, 92131 USA
1.619. 354. 2643 | www.readersmagnet.com

Book design copyright © 2022 by ReadersMagnet, LLC. All rights reserved.

Cover design by *Kent Gabutin*
Interior design by *Dorothy Lee*

Review/Praise

'J. M. Valente's BLOOD PASSION-Book Five~Rachael's Revenge is another fast-paced, engrossing Gothic Novel that cultivates your darkest thoughts and fears. You will dare not put down this book, for you are drawn to it as surely as a moth to a flame.

Rachael Valli, the stealthy, cunning, and hybrid human Vampire, has returned once again with a vengeance and a fury, the likes of which will leave the reader horrified and, yet, somewhat mesmerized. Rachael, nearly destroyed by her arch-nemesis, the U.S. Marshal Special Agent Angel Seraph, upends the tables in one heart-pounding, mind-boggling minute. Make no mistake, Rachael will destroy those who would stand in her way without a second thought. Together with her new love interest, Victor Vincent, they appear to be an unbeatable force and on a collision course with destiny in their pursuit of creating their very own; Vampire Cabal.

J. M. Valente, ever the highly skilled practitioner of the macabre storytelling, has once again successfully crafted this enthralling BLOOD PASSION fifth installment in his Novels Series, complete with a surprisingly shocking cliffhanger ending. That will defiantly stimulate and tantalize the reader's psyche.'

'A Spectacular Read!!'

Jeannie Scott Flynn

Acknowledgments:

Thanks once again,
to my Beta reader,
Jeannie Scott Flynn,
For keeping me inspired.
And a special thanks to
Ken Dodge Of Castalian Springs, TN.
For his inspiration for the Sub-Title,
and my Grammarly Editing Program,
& Amazon Fire Tablets.

Dedication:

*To my faithful Fans/Friends,
and to my absent
much-loved
Family members.*

TABLE OF CONTENTS

One 1
Two 5
Three 9
Four 13
Five 17
Six 21
Seven 24
Eight 28
Nine 33
Ten 37
Eleven 41
Twelve 45
Thirteen 49
Fourteen 54
Fifteen 58
Sixteen 63
Seventeen 67
Eighteen 72
Nineteen 76
Twenty 81
Twenty-One 85
Twenty-Two 89
Twenty-Three 93
Twenty-Four 98
Twenty-Five 102
Twenty-Six 106

Twenty-Seven	110
Twenty-Eight	114
Twenty-Nine	118
Thirty	123
Thirty-One	128
Thirty-Two	134
Thirty-Three	140
Thirty-Four	145
Thirty-Five	149
Thirty-Six	153
Thirty-Seven	157
Thirty-Eight	162

ONE

Mia Slowly Makes her way back to the New York City Plaza Hotel elevator area. Still feeling a little weak, she leans herself up against the wall, presses the up button, and impatiently waits for the elevator to arrive. The lift door finally slides open, she enters this empty elevator, somewhat unsteady on her feet, the lift operator notices, so displaying concern inquires,

"Pardon me, Ms. Are you all right?"

"Yes, I'm just fine, please. I just need to get to my room."

The operator requests,

"Floor, please?"

She replies, and the door closes. The elevator begins to rise swiftly. Stopping at her floor, she exits saying,

"Thanks!"

As she, slow but sure, makes her way to her room, she reflects,

This U.S. Marshal Seraph clearly wanted me dead for the taking of her sister's life, and she clearly could have killed me, but something stopped her. And she only knows me as the blond, blue-eyed Author Mia Harkness. Now would be the perfect time to return to my real name and identity, so glad I kept all my original identification stuff. I can now go back to being the brunette, hazel-eyed Rachael Valli of the town of Mystic.

She gets into her room, puts her phone on the bedside table, lollops into the bed to get some more much-needed rest. Closing her eyes, she quickly falls off to sleep. She hears someone calling to her, using her real name,

"Rachael, Rachael Valli."

She sluggishly leans up on her elbows to observe an undulating shadowy figure, with some things protruding out from behind it, standing at the foot of her bed, she inquires softly uttering,

"Who are…?"

A voice from this shadow interrupts her. It sounds somewhat familiar, but still quite strange,

"Rachael, the motorcycle you were driving is still in the Park. It's under the LaGuardia walkway bridge. I moved it there for you. I do believe it is still in working order."

Sleepily she answers,

"Huh, oh, yeah, my Bike, I will need it, I suppose I should say, thanks. But, wait, who… who are you?"

"I was sent to you in the Park, to right a wrong that had been done, what she did, or was trying to do to you, is forbidden. I wasn't in time to stop her, but I was in time to save you."

"As I said, I should thank you, but…."

"I know what you are going to say; that I saved a life that is cursed; maybe you'd be better off if I had just let you die."

"Exactly!"

"All life is precious; no matter what kind it is, it is a Gift. It is the Greatest Gift!"

"Well, my Gift, as you put it, is one of horror and dread. Do you know what I am? You must!"

"Yes, we do know what you are, and how you came to be, and what you are compelled to do to survive, and it was put upon you unintentionally, you are the love child of a Vampire, your father, and a Human, your mother, they had no idea what they would be creating, and this can not be undone, now I'm sorry but you will, and must live the life you were born to."

"You are… you're… sorry?"

"Yes, because there is no way to change what you are, it is not within, the powers that be, to alter you, from what you were born to be, again I'm sorry, there is nothing that can be done about it."

"Oh, well then, I guess I should thank you for saving my life."

"You are welcome. Just live it the best that you can, is all I can ask in the return of your gratefulness to us."

"Yes, yeah, okay. Us?"

Suddenly her Cellphone on the bedside table rings and wakes her. She opens her eyes, slowly sits up, and answers it,

"Hello?"

"Yes, hello, Ms. Harkness?"

"Yes, who's cal…?"

"It is Ms. Able from your Publisher, calling to remind you of your last book signing appearance in Boston this coming weekend. So, how did the New York one go?"

"Just great, and thanks for calling. Not to worry, I'll be there."

"Good, safe journey!"

"Yes, thanks, goodbye."

She hangs up, looks at the Cellphone to get what day it is. She thinks,

I've some time before I need to leave New York City for Boston, so I'll go get my Bike, take myself a ride along the waterfront tonight. I surely could use a Blood Passion feeding. This one in Boston is the last of my signing tour, so I'll get back to being who I really am and then find out who this Mr. Victor Vincent is. Oh, Rachael, you can be so bad, bad bad bad. But I need what I need!

In the early evening, she finds her red Honda Shadow Motorcycle lying under the bridge, just where she was told it would be. She takes a look around and sees that no one is about at the moment, so she brings out her Vampire powers, giving her the strength she needs to lift it up. It looks okay, so she mounts it, starts it up, takes the red, full-face tinted Helmet from the handlebars, and puts it on. Slowly now, she drives it out to the street. It's a little too early to cruise the harbor, so she'll take a spin around the City. As she's casually cruising, the U.S. Marshal, Angel Seraph, -that would have liked to destroy her, but only assaulted her with deadly force, then left her there in Central Park unconscious, for when the sun came up, it would finish her off, -walking with her Man, this Mr. Victor Vincent, together on the sidewalk of the street, she is riding on, observing them she speeds up and rides passed them, as no more than a red blur. Angel catches sight of this Bike and Rider, thinking,

No… could ant' be? I'd reckoned the sun musta' destroyed her. No one could have shown up to help her. I havta' figga' there are plenty ah red Motorcycles in this here big City. So that ain't her.

Victor takes note of Angel's deep in thought silence, so asks,

"Angel, why yuh so quiet? Somethin' on your mind?"

"No, my love, ain't nothin' on my mind, just enjoyin' my walk with you here in 'The Big Apple'!"

"So my love, any of them there secret assignments comin' for yah any time soon?"

"No, my sweet, they didna' say there was any when I met with them this here mornin'. I'll just call em' tomorrow."

"Good, that's ah meanin' we have tonight to…."

Before he can finish, she cuts him off,

"Oh, me oh my… my dear Mr. Victor Vincent, yah can be a mite devilish at times!"

"Yup, I can, yawl complainin'?"

"Not at all, Sir! Not one bit!"

"Good! Let's get us a drink in the Plaza Hotel Lounge."

"Yup, I'm a surely like in', that idea!"

TWO

Mia Slowly Cruises along the New York City Waterfront District. It's not quite nightfall yet, but the sun is getting low in the sky, no need for her night vision right now. So she will scope out the lay of this borough, checking out just where the deviants hang out. Then she will return when it is darker to find and acquire herself a reluctant Blood donor for her much-needed Blood Passion, hence replenishing her strength back to what it was before her encounter in Central Park with the U.S. Marshal, Special Agent, Angel Seraph. She will need to be at her full strength capacity before heading to Boston for her last appearance as Mia Harkness. Then, it will be adios' Mia Harkness. Welcome back, Rachael Valli.

She must, and she will find a way to bring Rachael Valli back into the world, so she contemplates,

Just as I had successfully planned and accomplished a way of faking my death, and disappearing, back there in Mystic, when I was under the assumption that the authorities were closing in on me, now I need to, somehow, do the reverse. All that, I'll strategize it out later, after I get my much-needed Blood Passion Feeding, while I'm making my way up to Boston.

It will be dark enough, very soon now, for her to find a victim for her Blood Passion feeding. So for now, she just cruises around the City, killing time before it's her 'Killing Time'. Then check out and then make her way north, off to Boston, to check-in at a place, she will call for a room reservation for one, maybe two nights

After a lovely room service dinner for herself and her Man, Angel gets a call from the U.S. Marshal's Washington DC Office; she answers,

"Hello? This is Special Agent, Angel Seraph!"

"Yes, we have Director Hughes. He is waiting for you. Please hold."

As she brings the phone away from her ear, Victor asks,

"What is it that you think they want?"

"A call at this hour; it must be something urgent."

Just as she brings the phone back to her ear, she hears,

"Angel, hello, sorry to call so late, but we've something that needs your attention asap! We have received a severe request for your presence in Paris, France.

I have our jet on standby, and as usual, I'll send you the details before you take off, so you can study it on your flight over there, and of course, you can bring your Bike. So what do you think?"

"What do I think? Just hold on, please."

She lowers the phone giving Victor an inquisitive look, and asks of him,

"Hey, my lover man, would ya like to go to France with me? I have an assignment over there; please say yawl will come."

"Well, I will have till next week to get back to work," and with a slight hesitation, he answers her,

"Heck yeah, I'd love to go!"

"Great! Start packing. We leave immediately!"

She puts the phone up to her mouth and says,

"Director, I'll gladly take this hear assignment, just as long as I can take my Victor with me."

"Angel, my dear, no need for you to ask that. Of course, you can. The plane is waiting at JFK, with all the usual clearances. Have a safe flight."

"Thank you, Sir. I'll be checking for your info E-mail at the Airport before we board. Can you tell me now anything of what it's about?"

"Well, all I can say right now is that it has to do with something they referred to as the 'Nightstalker'!"

Now being dark enough, Mia heads over to New York's Waterfront to acquire what she seriously needs.

She spots what appears to be alone deviant standing by a barrel on a small, rather dark pier, with water on both sides of it. She parks her Bike close by, and as she slowly walks toward him, she brings out her Vampire night vision to see that, yes, he is exactly what she needs. As she walks by without looking at him, he does notice that she is a young woman and inquires of her,

"Hey there, young woman, what yeah doing in this part of the City at this hour? It's not a good or safe place for anyone to be in at night!"

Without turning her head in his direction, she brings out her other Vampire attributes and says,

"Yes, I can see that, and I'll be delighted to show you why!"

Now, she turns around to notice that he has not turned to be facing her, so she swiftly comes up from behind him. Quickly wrapping her left arm around his neck, bending him back and down toward her, holding him fast, she places her right hand on his forehead, pulling his head back, and to the side, to get a clear opening to his neck, so she can quickly sink her fangs into his flesh, and faster than ever before, sucks in all of his Blood. As this now used body goes limp in her arms, she moves over to the edge of the pier, where she can just let go to let it fall into the water. With this done, she shifts her clothing and listens to hear anything that could threaten her. With her strength now replenished and feeling very confident, she laughs and thinks,

Like anything in this City could ever be a threat to me now at this time when I now have back my restored full Vampire abilities that I can bring out when needed.

With these thoughts, she relaxes to let her return to her Human look of Mia Harkness. Noticing her image in the moonlit water, she scours at her reflection, then goes to where her Bike is parked, gets to the Plaza Hotel, packs up, checks out, and leaves New York City for Boston.

After packing, she calls a prominent Hotel in Downtown Boston for a room for two nights.

As she now makes her way out of the City, ironically, her Bike and Angel's Bike pass each other on the street, speeding off opposite directions. After they pass by one another, Mia has; what she hopes, is a final thought concerning Angel,

She may believe she has destroyed the Vampire, Mia Harkness, but she has as of yet, to meet the Vampire,

Rachael Valli!

THREE

Mia Cruises On the highway north, in the general direction of Boston, Massachusetts. She should arrive by morning, check into her room to get a short nap, and then go to the Barnes and Noble bookstore signing. She will be on the lookout for Angel, just in case she knows about this event, it now being her last one on this Tour. In which, after she will make her way back to the Riverside Bed and Breakfast in Sleepy Hollow, in upper state New York, via Mystic, Connecticut to trade in the Bike for a Car at the Mystic Motors Dealership.

Since she has already informed the B & B, telling the manager Michael that her cousin Rachael will be taking her room, and the salesman, Frank at the Dealership, that she is coming to trade in the Bike for a car.

The U.S. Marshal's jet lands at the Paris, France airport where Angel and Victor disembark. They now wait on the tarmac for the cargo doors to be opened to access her Bike. After a quick dispensation through French Customs, they will ride to the Plaza Hotel, Paris, to check-in. Come the morning.

She will appear at the City Police Station for a briefing with the Captain and the Officers that are in charge of this so-called, strange 'Nightstalker' case. But for tonight, they will enjoy a delightful French meal at a quaint Bistro she knows of.

And then a restful night's sleep, for her meeting is in the morning.

Mia has now finished with the decent sales and uneventful book signing in Boston, goes to her hotel room for some room service, ordered dinner, and a few hours of sleep, for in the early morning, she will get on the road to Mystic.

She wakes early, checks out, and then goes to the parking garage to get her Bike, begins her trip south.

Angel enters the Paris police station at mid-morning and, in French, proceeds to announce to the desk Officer that she is the U.S. Marshal, Special Agent, Angel Seraph, here for a pre-arranged meeting with their Captain.

The Captain is called for, and he appears promptly, greets her respectively, then escorts her to his Office, stands behind his desk chair until she takes a seat. Angel settles in, so the Captain sits and produces from his desk the case file folder. And hands it to her announcing, in English,

"We've had it translated to English, just in case you do not read French."

"I do read a bit of French, but I do appreciate it bein' in English. It do make it, a might easier fir me."

She takes a few minutes to look it over and reacts,

"It sure does, looks to me, like yawl is under the impression that this here person is a Vampire or they believes they is."

"Yes, Marshal Seraph, as it says in the report, people show up here, or at the hospital with bite marks on their neck, or claimed they had been attacked by someone trying to bite them on the neck, for us that constitutes an alleged Vampire attack. Now would you not agree?"

"No, no, Sir, I agree, and please, it's Angel, ain't no reason to be so formal with me."

"Yes, of course, my dear, if you wish Angel, it shall be, and if you please, I'd like it if you would address me by my Christian name of Philippe."

"I sure can be ah doin' that fir yeah, Captain Philippe. Now I will need a drawn map of where this here perp has made their assaults, and I'd be a needin' to speak to your Offices that have been ah workin' on this, this here, as yous calls it, 'Nightstalker' case!"

As they leave the Office, Angel has a thought,

Maybe, just might be, I've got me another real one.

Still, as Mia Harkness arrives at the Mystic Motors Auto Dealership a little after noontime, Frank has all the paperwork set up for the trade-in and a vehicle type she requested waiting. With the paperwork signed and some moneys exchanged, she gets on her way to Sleepy Hollow, New York. While driving, she thinks,

I'll stop somewhere and change back to my brunette, hazel-eyed real self of Rachael Valli. Mia Harkness, a blue-eyed blonde, will be an uneventful resurrection from what I look like now. Although it will be nice to see Mike and young Benjamin again, I must act as if I have never met them, knowing about them and the place only from what my cousin, Mia, has told me about them, this could be fun. But I can't mess this up.

Rachael parks in the lot and makes her way to the Lobby, where Mike is behind the check-in counter doing his thing.

She approaches the desk and asks,

"You must be Mike?"

"And you, my dear, must be Mia Harknesses' cousin Rachael Valli. It's very nice to meet you. You do look a lot like Mia; if not for the Brown hair and Hazel eyes, you could be twins."

"Yeah, we get that a lot!"

"Well, the room is ready for you. I'll have Ben take you up. Now, where is that boy?"

Mike comes out from behind the counter, goes to the Dining room archway, and lets out a holler for Ben, Cathy, the dining room hostess, shows up, telling him that he is out front, and she will go to get him. In a minute, Ben shows up in the Lobby and is awestruck by how Rachael looks a lot like Mia. He starts to say something, but Mike cuts him off,

"Ben, yes, she does look similar to Mia. After all, they are cousins; now, just take her up to the room. Here is the key."

She turns to Mike and asks,

"Mike, don't you want me to sign in or something?"

"Yeah, I guess you should, but I'll just make a note that you will be occupying Mias' pre-paid room."

With her small overnight bag and computer case in tow, she follows Ben up to the room. At the room door, before he unlocks it, he asks of her,

"Will your cousin Mia be coming back here?"

"It's not likely. Her book is doing so well. She has gone to Europe to do signings over there. She even said something about staying over there to do some more writings."

"You mean like a sequel to her book. It is awesomeness!"

"Not sure of that, but maybe."

He unlocks and opens the door for her. As she walks in, she has a pleasant thought,

Wow, it feels like I never left.

As she hands him a tip, she says,

"Here you go, young Man, and thanks… it's Ben. Right?"

"Yup, you need or want anything, you just ask for Ben!"

"Yes, Mia told me how helpful you can be."

"And she was right, you'll see! Dinner is served around six; see you later!"

"Yes… Ben, I do believe I will, be seeing you later."

FOUR

Rachael Begins To settle back into the room she had occupied as her alias Mia Harkness. She checks the place where she had hidden most of her money, to be relieved that it is all there, and thinks,

I really should open a Bank account with a Debit card at a nearby Bank that has branches throughout the State of New York and beyond. I will talk to Michael, I mean Mike, for his advice on doing this. But first, I really need to give it a good counting.

I will only deposit enough at a time to live on, don't want to draw attention to myself financially, telling anyone, that may get too curious, that my cousin Mia Harkness, the Author, while away in Europe, is having a portion of her book royalties sent to me, of which she has arranged with her Publisher to do so.

Later today, I'll start searching the internet for this Victor Vincent person that the U.S. Marshall Angel Seraph that shot me and then left me for dead in Central Park, New York City, is sweet on. Come to think of it, wouldn't it be the perfect revenge to use my female wilds to beguile him and do a turning making him a Vampire like me. Oh yeah, her being, the Hunter of the Supernatural, for the US Marshalls' Department, such as Vampires and the like, would have to hunt the Man she loves to his possible demise. I would have ta' say, that would be some real sweet revenge for her trying to destroy me.

After giving the money a good counting, to find she still has quite a bit left, and more coming from the royalties she arranged to have sent to her from the Publisher for her novel written in her Mia Harkness cousin, disguise.

After Rachael dresses for the day, she heads down to have a late light breakfast and speak with Mike about the banking stuff.

In the Lobby, she's greeted by young Benjamin, who is habitually full of questions.

"Good morning, Rachael Valli!"

"Good morning, Ben. Is Mike around?"

"Yes, I believe he's in the Kitchen talking with his sister, our chef Jeannie! Do you want me to get him for you?"

"No, Ben, I can wait till he comes out."

"Is there something I can help you with?"

"No, Ben, I just want to speak with him, just need to ask him something."

"All righty then." Ben states and asks as he sits on the lobby bench, "So, how ya liking it round here?"

"So far, I like it just fine. It's real quiet."

"Yup, sometimes a little too quiet for me."

"I suppose it would be for a teenager."

Just then, Mike enters the Lobby, as usual drying his hands on a Kitchen towel, putting it on the shelf behind the counter, and addresses Rachael.

"Morning, Miss Valli. Can I be of any help?"

"Well, yes, but first, I'd like it if you and Ben would address me by my first name of Rachael, and yes, you can help me, I hope."

"So, just what is it you are hoping that I can help you with?"

"Just need to open a Bank account, with one around here, that would have branches throughout the state and possibly beyond."

"Oh yeah, I can help you with that, no problem. I will get you the info while you have your breakfast. Okay?"

As she's passing through the archway into the dining room, she answers him,

"Good, see you then after I eat."

After her light breakfast, Rachael goes into the Lobby to see Mike. He is at the counter dealing with a new lodger. She takes a seat on the lobby bench to await his attention. Mike signals her to wait a moment; she nods in agreement.

Mike now concluded with the new occupant, and with Ben now escorting them up to their room, he can now attend to Rachael to help her with what it is that she had wished of him.

"So, okay, Rachael, so you want to open a bank account?"

She rises from the bench and addresses him.

"Yeah, Mike, as I said before, I would like to know if there is a good bank nearby that I can open up an account with. I like it to have branches."

"Well, yes, there is, the one we use can accommodate you very nicely, I believe. And it is nearby," as he hands her the written information, he says, "so here you go."

She accepts his note with gratitude, saying,

"Thanks, I'll give them a call asap!"

As she ascends the stairs, she passes Ben. He asks of her,

"You all set with what you needed from Mike?"

"Yup! See you later, Ben."

"Okey Dokey, later!"

Now in her room, she enters the Bank info into her Cellphone. Not wanting to go and take care of it today, she has already decided to go to the small ladies' clothing shop, up on the main road, where she had patronized in her alter identity of Mia Harkness. After a pleasant, leisurely walk up to the Main Road, she enters the shop and is right away greeted by a lovely young, fair-haired girl,

"Why hey there, good aftanoon, Miss. Yous' ah lookin' for anythin' in particula'?"

Rachael has a reminiscing thought:

Rose is still here. Her aunt, the owner, Anna Beth, must still be in ill health.

"You must be Rose. I am Rachael Valli, cousin to someone you just may remember."

"Well, cusein' me, and just who mite your cousin be?"

"Do you at all remember Mia Harkness? I believe she frequented this shop once or twice."

"Yup, I sures do. Whert' she an Author?"

Rachael has a quick thought,

You have to love that southern accent of hers.

"Yes, Rose, she is a published Author, now touring Europe with her first Novelette, so I'm residing in her prepaid room at the Riverside Inn, she was staying at, down on Riverside Road."

"Yup, I do's rememba' her, lovely lady. She shopped with us a few times. And mite I be ah sayins', you do's looks a lot like her, but she had blonde hair like mines, and blue eyes, I do believes."

"Yes, she did, but we have the same facial features. Everyone says so. You could say we are identical cousins."

"I ain't neva' seen that happen before, but likein' my aunt Anna Beth is ah always ah saying anythin' is possible, on this here Gods' green Earth."

"So's, Miss Rachael, anythin' I can hep you to be ah findin'?"

"Yes, maybe; I need some new intimates."

"Yup, well, we haves' a fine selection, here lets me shows yawl, right over ta here."

So Rachael finds what she needs and a few things she likes. Leaving the shop, she thanks Rose for all her help. In making her way back to the Inn, she takes a short detour stroll along the Hudson River Bank, where she gets a little lost in her thoughts of when she was known here in Sleepy Hollow as Mia Harkness.

FIVE

Rachael Enters The Lobby of the River Side Inn with her shopping bags. Mike takes notice and observes,

"So, I see you have done a little shopping today."

"Yup, walked up to Anna Beth's Ladies Shop, cousin Mia told me about it, it's a nice little shop, and the shop girl, Rose, is very obliging!"

"Anna Beth, wasn't there?"

Mike inquires.

"No, I was also told about her not being in good health."

"Yup, I spoke with my brother, Pete, recently, and he said his wife is not doing well."

"That's too bad. I hope she recovers soon."

"We all do. She's a lovely southern woman."

"I do believe my cousin told me she's from somewhere in Alabama."

"Yeah, not sure, but I think it was Mobile."

Mike finishes.

"Well, I'm going up now to put these things I bought away. See you at dinner."

"Yup, see ya then, dear."

Up in her room, after putting the new items away, she opens her laptop Computer with a glass of Wine she had left there as Mia, to

Google Victor Vincent and learn all she can about him. After finding that he is an appropriator of historical artifacts at the Smithsonian in Washington, DC, and lives in Atlanta, Georgia.

She now begins to feel a little fatigued and remembers that it has been a while since her last Blood Passion feeding, so a little trip up to the 'Horseman Tavern' just may be needed this evening.

After a short nap, and a nice hot shower, and fixing her hair and makeup, she chooses something a little provocative to wear. It is a beautiful Bella Luna night, so after she has her dinner, she will take a stroll up to the main road, where the tavern location is not too far from the A B Ladies shop, before entering. She stops to think,

I do remember the bartender's name is Joe, but I will play dumb and act like I do not know his name.

Taking a seat at the bar, she scans the room for an unsuspecting victim, which does not take long at all to find one, because they usually find her, and sure enough, as she gets settled, a middle-aged man seats himself next to her in the empty barstool, announcing as he gestures to the bartender,

"Good evening! May I be granted the pleasure of buying you a drink?"

"Yes, you may. I am Rachael. I will have a glass of Red Wine."

"I'm Frank. It is very nice to meet you, Rachael."

He then acquires the full attention of the barkeep by declaring,

"Joe, please a glass of Red Wine for the Lady, and I'll have another Beer, and it will be on my tab, thank you."

Joe response,

"Coming right up!"

As they wait for their drink order,

"So, Frank, you live round here?"

"No, just passing through by train, on business."

She lowers her head and smiles with a quick thought,

Perfect, he's just what I need tonight.

He curiously smiles back at her as their drinks are delivered. Rachael picks up hers to take a sip,

"Yum, that is good! It was a little warm today, but the night has cooled down nicely now. It's become a truly nice night to take a stroll along the Hudson River."

"My thoughts exactly!"

He replies and continues questioningly,

"So, shall we?"

"I'd say yes, right after we finish our drinks."

"Oh yes, by all means, please do enjoy your Wine first."

After a bit more small talk and having finished their drinks, Frank pays the tab in cash and leaves to head down to the River. The Full Moon's undulating reflection on the water is somewhat hypnotizing. They leisurely walk along until they enter a small clearing that Rachel recognizes from past feedings. Putting her back up against a tree, she smiles flirtatiously. As Frank comes in closer, she looks up at him.

"I just love it here!"

"Yes, it is rather nice and calming here."

Frank agrees as he leans in to steal a kiss from her.

Rachael turns her face away, so he turns his to try to make contact with her lips. Quickly she throws her arms about him, holding him fast, now turning her face in the other direction away from him so as her Vampire attributes of red eyes, fangs, and extended fingernails appear unseen by him, with his head turned away from her, and his neck clearly exposed. She bites him and commences to feed quickly on his hot Blood so quickly that he's not able to utter a sound, weakening him to the point of no resistance whatsoever.

She relieves him of any of his identification. She finishes this much-needed feeding, which never really takes no time at all, letting go of his now lifeless body, where it falls to the ground. Taking the time to replenish her powers, then picks up the body to put it into the River and his trappings slightly after.

Looking at her reflection in the water to check for any telltale signs of her vital to her existence endeavor, she has now performed countless times with very little remorse. After shifting and clearing her clothing of any debris, she begins to make her way back to the

Inn. As she casually strolls along, her Vampire appearance diminishes back to her Human form, and she smiles, with the callous thought of,

Yes, Frank, the waters of the Hudson are very calming in death, um, I mean indeed.

As she enters the Lobby, Mike looks up from the counter and welcomes her back,

"Good evening, my dear. Having a nice night?"

As she ascends the stairs, she answers him back,

"Yes, very, thanks, good night!"

He replies,

"Yup, I will see you tomorrow."

And he goes back to what he was doing.

SIX

ANGEL CRUISES THE area of Paris, France, in the daylight, that she was told this 'Nightstalker' had been spotted. Its intended victims claim it attacked or endeavored to assault them. Also, she checks out the place where a passerby discovered the dead victim. Near this place, she takes notice of what she assumes is a neglected old Gothic Cathedral, she thinks,

Possibly where this Stalker thing abodes itself.

She pulls her Harley over and parks it. She takes her Shotgun from the front fork and slowly ascends the stairs to the large double front doors. She pushes with one hand, but it does not yield, shouldering her weapon, and with two hands now, she finds that both doors, loudly creaking, submitting to her vigor. She cautiously enters this dark and dank place, only lit by the sun's rays emanating through the large stained glass windows. She jerks a little when she hears what appears to be large black wings flapping, way up in the high arching ceiling. She looks up at it and proclaims to this thing,

"Well, I'd reckon you for sure lives here if only you could talks to me. Sure enough, would makes my job a mite easier iffins' yawl could."

With her weapon at the ready, she slowly walks the broad center aisle looking and listening for anything that could be a threat, not too sure what it might be, so she stays vigil. Stopping at the three steps that lead up to the Altar, she walks up and takes notice of a large stain, strangely illuminated by a single ray of sunlight, on the white covering. It looks to her to be Blood. She is somewhat amazed, claiming,

"Dang! Can it, could it, be… Blood?"

She takes out her cell phone to get a picture of it and show it to the Police Captain and his men.

Back at the station now, she sits alone in an Office, waiting for the Captain and the two Officers originally assigned to the case. The Captain shows up first, sits down, and asks,

"So, Marshall, what had your preliminary observations found?"

"Before I speak, it would be best iffin' your Officers should hear about my findins.'"

When the two Officers show up, she reports what she found, showing them the picture on her phone, telling them how she wants to go about apprehending this so-called 'Nightstalker'. Making it clear to them, it will be better if she handles it alone. The Captain agrees, and so do his men. She tells them as she's leaving the room,

"I'll be a goins' back alone tonight after my dinner with Victor and see if there is any action."

After a lovely dinner in a quaint Bistro on the avenue with her lover Victor, they stroll back to the Plaza Hotel, and with a deep emotional kiss, she leaves him, to go do her job. He, of course, wishes her safe.

She parks the Bike about two blocks away from the old Cathedral, armed with her 45 magnum loaded with silver bullets and a solid silver knife. She stations herself in the shadows across the street from the front doors. It is only pure luck that a full moon illuminated the front of this gothic structure, making it easier for her to see if there is any movement in or out.

Just as she notices one of the doors begin to open, a police car goes screaming by with its siren blasting. As the vehicle goes by, the door closes. When things become quiet, one of the doors starts to open once again. She backs deeper into the shadows watching this thing or person emerge wearing what looks like a long black hooded shiny cloak. As it ascends the large staircase and begins to walk down the sidewalk, she notices that it seems to float along, or is it just a trick of the dim lighting, coupled with the fact that what they are wearing is hiding their legs. She stealthily follows from a safe distance, so as not to be noticed by it, quietly, slowly gaining on it, as she comes within range of her weapon, she announces loudly,

"All right, you, freeze and do not turn round!"

It turns swiftly on a dime, and from under its cloak, it throws something to the ground that produces a flash and a cloud of smoke. In what seems to happen in an instant, it somehow disappears. Angel stands slightly dismayed with surprise thinking,

Okay, sure enough never seen that one before, but like I usually says, I should always expect the unexpected. This one caught me a little off my guard. Am I losing my edge? Where it disappeared to I do not have a clue; unfortunately, I don't know this City very well. Sos' I'll just call it a night and try another night again. Next time I'll try to be inside where it won't expect me to be.

She lowers her weapon, turns round, and begins to walk back to where she parked her Bike, mounts, and slowly drives back to the Hotel looking for anything suspicious, but sees nothing she can deem unusual.

Victor is profoundly pleased to see that she is back safe and sound. She sadly tells him of the failed encounter.

With his hands tenderly placed on her shoulders, he can only think of saying, along with a kiss on her forehead,

"Better luck next time, my Love."

With that, they settle down for a night's rest.

Back at the Cathedral, from the top of the Centre Turret, shown by the full moon's light. A large black, winged creature flies out into the night sky.

SEVEN

RACHAEL WAKES AT ten in the morning uses the Bathroom to get herself ready to go down for a little breakfast. After enjoying her lite breakfast, and some lite hearted conversation with Ben, about her, supposed cousin Mia' Vampire book 'Mystic Vampyres', and listening to his adorations about how much he loved it, also stating that he would love for her to write some more.

"Well, Ben, she is over in Europe right now; just maybe she will write some more of it while over there."

At that, Ben stands up, excitedly proclaiming,

"Oh, my God! That would be so awesome! Will you let me know if she is going to? Please."

"Of course, I will, Ben."

"Thanks, Rachael. I think they need me in the Kitchen; you have yourself an awesome day now! See you later, and never forget if you need anything, anything at all, just call on me."

"Okay, you have an awesome day too."

Mike comes to her table, as she is finishing her cup of Irish Breakfast Tea, asking,

"Would you like some more tea, my dear?"

"No thanks, I had my fill for now. Have some things to do on my computer, so I'll see you later."

Up in her room, she opens her Laptop to get the Smithsonian phone number in DC. She dials the number, and a woman's voice answers,

"Good day, Smithsonian Institution. How may I help you?"

"Yes, you might. I am looking to speak with an ah… Mr. Victor Vincent."

"I'm sorry, but he is out of the country at the moment. May I take a message? He does call in, from time to time."

"Oh no, no message. Do you happen to know when he is due back?"

"That I am not too sure of, he does go on these trips quite a bit, he is somewhat of a world traveler for his job here, so he just may be back rather soon; you could try back in a day or so."

"Thanks, I will, bye."

She hangs up and thinks,

Okay, so now I know he definitely does work there, and now, this will give me more time to find a good reason to approach him. I think in the meantime, I will take myself a little trip to New York City. I will let Mike know, so he will not be concerned if I am gone for a day or so.

In their room, at the Paris Plaza, while having their breakfast, Victor tells Angel that he must be getting back stateside soon. She tells him if he must go, then he should because she's not sure how much longer she will be needed to stay, assisting the French Police in this case.

He books the very next commercial flight back, the plane lands in Washington DC, and he goes right to the Smithsonian to notify them that he is back, and check on a few exhibits he is in charge of, the receptionist informs him of a call from a woman, about a day ago. He inquires of her,

"Did she leave her name?"

"No, she did not, but I told her to call back in a few days."

"Okay, thank you, Meghan; I will be in my Office for most of the day so that you can transfer any of my calls there, as usual."

"Yes Sir, nice to have you back safe!" and she thinks,

Oh, my God! What a hunk that Man is!

Back in Paris, Angel sets out in the early evening; she will do a steak-out in the Cathedral for her second try to apprehend this deviant. After checking the other entries and exits to find they all are secure with chains and padlocks, it seems that the front doors are the only way in or out. She waits fully armed, about an hour or so, hiding herself between the pews at the front doors where she saw this so-called 'NightStalker' come out. The only thing she has heard or seen so far is the Creature that is up in the ceiling rafters—thinking and hoping that this so-called 'NightStalker' has not relocated themselves after their first encounter.

Failing on her first try, which does not happen very often, usually makes the suspect move to a new location. If that is the situation, this will take her a lot longer to complete the case and return home.

She has now waited almost all night, feeling that this is not going to happen tonight. She decides to go back to her Hotel and wait for some more Intel from the Police reportings. Vigilantly and unobtrusively, after doing a stealthy walk-through, she leaves this old Gothic Cathedral. She will do another daytime reconnaissance tomorrow. She needs to familiarize herself with the area a little more, and maybe talking with the locals will bring her some information she could use.

In the mid-afternoon, Rachael packs a small bag for her trip to the 'Big Apple'. After informing Mike of her trip, she fills her car's tank and gets on the road heading for New York City. She heads for the Plaza Hotel, where she had stayed, as her alter self Mia Harkness. After dinner, she acquires a room and gets settled in; she will have a stroll in downtown Manhattan.

Now, having dined in the hotel restaurant, she heads out for her stroll. After she had walked a few blocks, she has changed her mind about walking, so she jumps in a Cab that is waiting right in front of the Community College in Manhatten for a fare. This Cabby turns round to her and announces,

"Excuse me, Miss, but this Cab is taken. I'm just now waiting for the customer!"

She hopefully retorts,

"Maybe, they won't mind sharing?"

The Cab driver tolerantly replies,

"Maybe, we will see."

She moves over to the far side, behind the driver, turns her head to look out at the street to watch the people walking on the other side of the avenue. Within a few moments, a person opens the door and begins to get in, immediately they take notice of a person already in the Taxi, and they demandingly proclaim,

"Excuse me, but this is my Taxi Cab!"

Without turning her head to see who it is, Rachael recognizes the voice of her longtime childhood friend and so replies with the inquisitive rhetorical statement,

"So, Lucy, what, you now own your own, Taxi Cab."

"Oh, my God! Rachael, is it... is it you?"

Racheal immediately turns to her. Lucy excitedly declares,

"It's you! Yes, I just knew you weren't dead. It wasn't just a wishful dream; I was right! Oh my God, It was you! It so was you that did the book signing as the Author Mia Harkness here in New York City!"

They immediately hug, and Lucy starts to cry tears of joy.

Racheal admits,

"Yes, Lucy, It's me, your old friend, alive and well!"

Lucy inquisitively exclaims,

"You will please tell me all about what happened to you and why?"

"Yes, I will, Lucy, but not here in this Cab."

"If not here, then where?"

The Cabby just sits, somewhat puzzled at what he sees and hears, watching them in his rearview mirror. He gives them a moment, then hesitantly inquires of them,

"So, ladies, where to?"

EIGHT

Lucy Responds To the Cab driver,
"The Coffee Pot at 403 W 51st Street, please."
As the Cabby pulls out into traffic he, just replies,
"Yes, Ms., coming right up."
She then turns to Rachael and explains,
"It's where all the students go! They have the most choice coffee and an awesome variety of tea in Manhattan, pastry, and stuff! And yes, we can talk privately there, as well."
All Rachael can say, for now, is,
"Kool Beans, Lucy."
In the Manhattan traffic, it takes roughly fifteen minutes to get there, which gives Rachael some time to think of what she can tell Lucy about what took place back in Mystic, those many months ago, she ruminates,
I will need to lie to her because the truth would only freak her out, so deceiving her can be the only way to proceed. It's bad enough that Shane has learned the truth, and from that U.S. Marshal, to boot. Running into him, as I am now back to being my original self, he could easily recognize that it would be extremely awkward, at the least, to say the most.
They receive their coffee order and attain a small table off in a cozy corner of the shop. As they seat themselves, Rachael asks,
"So, Lucy, you're attending classes here in New York City now?"

"Yup, ain't it just, so much Kool Beans, as you would say! I went as far as I could in Connecticut, so when I was here in The Big Apple, following someone I believed was really you, and then I kinda' lost you, I enrolled in the Community College. Thinking maybe this is where you were living now."

"So you surmised, I was living here, in New York City?"

"Yup, why not? Isn't this where Shane lives?"

"Yes, he does, with his Wife!"

"What what! He got married?"

"Lucy, that is, how a man gets a Wife."

"I know that… Silly."

"Mmmm… this coffee is delicious!"

"So, Rach, you are, living in New York?"

"Sort of."

"What do you mean by, sort of?"

"Lucy, what I sort of mean is, upper state New York."

"You mean like, up in Albany?"

"No, not that much upper."

"Then, where in New York, Rachael, for criminy sake?"

"Lucy, still as nosy as ever, I see, well if you must know, in Terrytown on the Hudson River."

"Wait! Where Sleepy Hollow is, where the Headless…!"

Rachael cuts her off,

"Lucy, come on, there isn't any and has never been a Headless Horseman there. It's a totally fictional story."

"Okay, so, where'd you get to that night I caught up with you at the Barnes and Noble book store here in New York City, after finding you in Mystic first, at the Bank Square Bookstore, as the author Mia Harkness, of the book 'Mystic Vampyres'? Which I would have to say is pretty good!"

"I went to Boston, Massachusetts, for another signing, my last one on the tour."

"And thanks, my book is doing rather well."

"That is so awesome for you; congrats! So now, Rachael, where did you go when you left Mystic some time ago, and why did you leave?

You do realize everyone, including your poor grieving mother and Grandmother, beliefs you to be dead? It's one of the many enduring mysteries in the Town of Mystic, Connecticut!"

"Oh, really, Lucy, and just what are the others?"

"Well, the first and foremost one is; the mysterious disappearance of your real father, Michael Valli, and then there is also the vanishing of your mother's friend, your Godmother Marlena Varlino!"

Rachael humorously replies,

"I'd have to say; they are piling up, huh?"

"Rach, come on now, it's not funny."

Racheal takes a moment to think,

Oh boy, where do I start?

"Well, Lucy, do you remember that there was for a time in most of the Connecticut and Rhode Island newspapers, there being some very horrific reports of people, that were mostly homeless persons, being found dead in Hartford and in Providence with very little to no Blood in them?"

"Yup, now that was truly horrific; it was like there was a real Vampire running round our State and the State of Rhode Island! Everyone was locking their doors at night. I was locking my bedroom door and windows. So what's that got to do with your disappearance?"

"Okay, so, well, the Mystic Police were in the vacant lot next to my house looking for, I don't know what, but they found some animals in that similar condition."

"Oh my, they, they were dead too, with no, no Blood?"

"Yup, Lucy, okay, please calm down. Yes, they were dead. And you do recall that Monster thingy you encountered, out in the yard, the night of the Cliff House warming party. Right?"

"Oh, yup, how could I forget that? Way too scary! Do you think that it was that Monster thingy doing all those killings in Connecticut and in Rhode Island?"

"What I was thinking really didn't matter, it was what the Police were thinking that mattered to me, but I did overhear them from my Kitchen window, talking about approaching me, like I had something to do with it all."

"Oh, my, Rachael, but you didn't. Right?"

"Of course I didn't, I'm… I am not a Vampire. They were and are fictitious creations for books and movies."

Rachael chides herself, ruminating,

Liar, I.

"So was it that Monster thingy doing it all?"

"That I don't know, but I wasn't about to stick around to find out, so I quickly left in the night before that Monster thingy came for me."

"Oh, Rach, real scary stuff, so in that case, I don't blame you at all. But why the new identity and your death thing?"

"Lucy, you do always have more questions. Okay, well, if they thought I was dead, the Police wouldn't come looking for me."

"That worked out for you real good, but I found you, and I'm sure glad I did."

And with that said, they hug.

Lucy whispers into Rachael's ear,

"What about letting your mom and Grandmom, your Me-Ma that is, know about you being alive and well living here in New York State?"

"That, my dear Lucy, I will need to think about how to go about it without giving them too much of a shock!"

"Yup! Especially your Me-Ma."

"Yes, you're right about that, but if they are to know, it should only come from me. If you say something, they will think you have gone nuts with grief or something like it."

Rachael has a quick thought,

Letting them know that I'm not dead would only impede my plans for revenge, and I can not and will not let that happen.

In her mind, abruptly from nowhere, she hears, from a strange but seemingly familiar gravelly male voice these words,

'Exactly, my dear, you cannot let anything stop you.'

Instantly she looks around to see if anyone in the place is watching her. She softly says,

"Hello? Did someone just say something to me?"

Lucy hears her and replies,
"I didn't say or hear anyone talk to you?"
Rachael retorts,
"I just thought I... oh, never mind; I think I just need some air."
"All right, Rach, then let's take us a walk."

NINE

Angel Makes Sure that her Bike is in good working order and that her Weapons are loaded, secure, and in good operating service before she goes out later for tonight's excursion; with any and all of the latest Intel, she can obtain.

Tonight will be her second attempt to apprehend this so-called 'NightStalker'. She has now determined that after dinner, she will go to the neglected old Gothic Cathedral and once again do a stakeout of the place on the inside, all night if need be, till dawn, she is intensely anticipating a resolving showdown with whatever this elusive 'NightStalker' is, so she can close this case and get back to the States.

After having herself a light dinner so that a heavy French meal wouldn't slow her down, she makes her way to the Cathedral. After parking the Bike, as she ascends the large front stairs, she hears a strange loud screech from above, looking up to see briefly what looks to her like a large black object with wings, quickly flying into the Belfry. She reasons,

So that strange creature that is roosting in the tower is here.

She relays softly out loud,

"So me an that there creature thing again tonight, I reckon there just might be a connection, with that thing, and the 'NightStalker', wait just a doggone minute. What am I ah, thinking'? That would be an actual supernatural thing. Okay, girl, let's go see iffin' it's true?"

She, quietly as possible, opens the doors, and steps in swiftly moves to the last pew, which is the closest to the doors, knowing it's the only typical way in or out, and lays down on it, with her shotgun at the ready. She pokes her head up to get a good look round but sees nothing or no one. Once again, the full moon helps her see in the darkness, but she does have her night goggles in the saddlebag but failed to bring them in with her. After about thirty or so minutes, she hears a soft thud and then what she believes are footfalls coming down the center aisle. She thinks,

Was it in here? And heard, or seen me enter?

Just as her thoughts stop, so do the footsteps. She lays still breathing softly, as the footsteps start again, she slowly moves the shotgun out from under her, to be able to place her finger on the trigger at about the same time, this thing that is walking shows up and just stops, in the aisle at the end of the pew, that she is lying down in, waiting. Because of the awkward position she is in, she has a little trouble pulling back the hammer, but before it can lock, it slips off of her thumb, and the gun fires, auto rotates the magazine, and quickly fires again. Hearing this thing make a loud, high-pitched screech as it swiftly goes down to the floor. Having a prompt thought as she begins to rise to a seated position from the lying position she was in,

That there, autoload and fire feature, works dang well, must have had it engaged without ah knowin' it.

She gets herself up off the pew and comes to the place in the aisle, where the thing she hit went down. She turns on the flashlight in her phone only to see a shiny black cloak that appears to be more like some kind of skin lying spread out reasonably flat on the floor. She uses the Shotgun barrel to move it out of the way and only sees a shallow gathering of what looks to her as black ashes. Gets a picture of it for evidence, proclaiming,

"Gaul dang it, what do you know, it really was, somethin' supernatural, or more, to my likein', somethin' super-unnatural."

She just stands still, holding her breath, quietly listening for any sounds that may be a threat to her, like another one of those things being in here. She sits in the adjacent pew to the one she was lying in and continues to listen and watch. She is also taking some time to collect her thoughts and her wits. When she feels she has waited long enough, she picks up the cloak and leaves.

Outside now, the wind blows the cloak open, the full moonlight shines through the many, small holes made by the small silver balls in the two shells from the rapid Shotgun blasts that hit it, telling, and showing her that she actually did hit something that was solid, to begin with, and then mysteriously turned to black ashes. Placing the cloak in one of the Saddlebags and her Weapons securely away, she mounts her Bike and heads to the Hotel to get some sleep, to be well-rested for the report to the Captain and his men in the morning.

In the morning, after a call to the French Police Captain and a light breakfast of Coffee and a Croissant, she arrives at the station.

In their lot, she Parks her Harley, removes the cloak from the saddlebag, places it in her rucksack, and enters the Captain's Office. After about two minutes, the Captain and his men show up, asking her what happened. She gives them the run down and then pulls the cloak out, spreading it out on the floor. Their reaction is one of amazement and disbelief. After showing them the picture of the black ashes on the Cathedral floor, they start to become more accepting of her account of the incident.

The Captain leans forward to his desk, closes the file folder, then leans back in his desk chair and declares,

"Okay, so you did it, I just wish you had brought in some of the ashes, but I would have to say, you have done a heck of a job in two days, where we have been working on it for months," at that he stands up behind his desk, puts out his hand to her, she moves in to reciprocate, as he continues with, "Thank you, and as you would say in your part of the world, we sure do appreciate you, for coming here, now that this 'NightStalker' case is officially closed."

"Well, Captin', yous is welcome, and ya can just send one of ya men to collect some of them there ashes, iffin' ya really needs it, and ya do knows where it is."

As she talks to them, she texts a message to the pilot to get the plane ready to take her back to the States. His response to her text is; okay, in about two hours, we can take off.

"Well there, gentleman, it has been real, my plane goes in about two hours, so iffin' yous people evers needs me again just calls my Captin.'"

With that, she takes her leave of the Police station to get to her room and pack up to go home.

Later that afternoon, the Captain calls in one of the officers working the case to have him go and get some of the ashes. He goes in with a small scoop and an empty plastic pale and comes out a minute later with the scoop, but the pale is still empty. In his patrol car, he calls the Captain to inform him that he could not find any of the ashes. The Captain just answers him with,

"Well, Officer Franks, this bizarre case for us is still and now officially closed."

A few days later, when this derelict old Gothic Cathedral was to be torn down, the workmen doing a walkthrough were somewhat appalled to find what looked to them; to be some Human remains, up in the Belfry.

TEN

Lucy Walks With Rachael to the Plaza Hotel, where she is staying for her time in New York City. They stop at the front staircase, Rachael asks of her,

"Hey, Lucy, you want to come in the Hotel lounge to have a drink with me to celebrate our reunion?"

"Um, Rachael, I'd really love to, but I have some heavy studying to do for a really important exam tomorrow, sorry. Can I get a rain check on it?"

"Of course, you can. I'll be in the City for a few more days, so just call me, here I'll give you my cell number."

Lucy puts the number in her Cellphone and replies,

"Great, I'll call, and maybe on this Saturday we can do it."

"Well, I will be leaving the City on Sunday late morning, so that would be so fetch. See you then."

They hug with a mutual kiss on the cheek.

And as Lucy forlornly walks away, she imparts,

"Yup, you have a good night, bye."

As Rachael is ascending the staircase, she looks back and waves goodbye.

Rachael gets into the lift to go to her room to freshen up and change for dinner in the Hotels' Palm Court restaurant. After having her dinner, she takes a walk over to Central Park. She goes to the location where the memories come flooding back, when she, in her alter identity of Mia Harkness, had a physical, violent confrontation with that, U.S. Marshal Angel Seraph, in which the Marshal, shot her in the shoulder and then left her for dead. She places her hand on her shoulder where the wound was and continues to remember what happened next; then, like from nowhere, that mysterious shadowy entity appeared and saved me. She wonders if the Marshal believes she was destroyed. But if she does or doesn't, it would make no difference, because it was Mia, she would have believed she terminated not me, as my real self… Rachel Valli.

The memories of this event begin to make her feel angry, to the point where her eyes turn red, so she literally sees red. She turns on her heels and heads back to the Hotel, firmly deeming in her mind,

I WILL have my Revenge! I must begin to construct my detailed plan soon on just how to go about making unsuspecting contact with the Marshals' lover, Mr. Victor Vincent, to use as my catalyst for it, and maybe more.

Suddenly, that strange Voice she had heard earlier emanates piercingly, in her mind,

Yes, and I would be more than pleased to help you with that.

And just as abruptly, she spins round, thinking,

Who is…?

Seeing no one, she accelerates her pace back to the Hotel. And as she is speed walking, she surmises,

I must really be overtired, and my mind is playing tricks on me. I just need a good night's sleep.

In a dreadfully strange and extremely nefarious place, she can only see off in the distance two small points of faint light, getting closer, larger and brighter as they seem, to be coming towards her. These lights are not white or yellow. They have a red tinge to them, intensifying to a deep red as it comes closer.

Seemingly frozen with terror, she cannot move to escape this dreadful encounter with, what appears to her as two large red eyes, hovering in the darkness, right before her, suspended in midair, and suddenly the Voice she has been hearing in her mind, emanates once again.

Rachael, my dear sweet child, be not afraid. I am here to help you.

She has a remembrance thought,

I do remember my father's spirit, saying almost the exact words to me, in Marlena's Bedroom in the cliff house, the night I broke in.

With this memory, she becomes able to commune with this thing by using her mind, without her mouth moving, enquiring,

father... Marlena, is this either of you?

Well, my dear, you could say both.

Both?

Yes, both, because I cohabited with both of them at separate times, but of course, I believe you are aware of that fact.

Yo... You.... You are the spiritual essence of that mutated Bat that integrated into their minds and, at times, their bodies for the Blood Passion feedings!

Precisely, my child, your father christened me Malice Nightwing, while your Godmother, Marlena, entitled me to,

Menace Nightshade. I do believe that you, yourself unknowingly had named me, Malevolence Nightwing, Child of Malice, you being not really aware of me, because I was somewhat quiescent within you, I was restoring my mental powers and strength, just waiting for the right time to emerge within your psyche. My now diminished spiritual essence does not have the ability to control you as I did at times with your father and Marlena, but I can and will be able to psychologically advise you from time to time.

You would be with me in my mind, like a teacher, of sorts?

Precisely! Your loneliness is over.

Loneliness? A voice in my head is not a partner! I do have a plan not to be alone anymore.

I know.

You know?

Yes.

Enigmatically, coming from somewhere within this darkness, she realizes a phone is ringing, slowly growing louder and louder and finally waking her from sleep. Slowly opening her eyes, she rolls over to the night table, and ineptly procures the phone and sleepily answers,

"He… hello?"

"Good morning, Ms. Valli. This is the nine AM wake-up call you requested."

"Good morning, yes, I did, thank you!"

"It is partly cloudy and seventy degrees here in New York City. Have a wonderful day! Bye."

"Thanks again, I certainly will try to! Bye."

She hangs up and ruminates on her plan. In her mind,

I need to go shopping today to get a nice business-type suit and a briefcase, for when I go to the Smithsonian in DC and make contact with this Victor guy, I will need to look like a professional person with some interest in artifacts. Telling him something about a skull relic with fangs like a Vampire, found recently in Eastern Europe, should spark his interest in me and what he thinks I might know about it because the Smithsonian Internet Site informed me that he is the Curator of the Historical Artefacts Department. That must be why he travels so much. I plan on being in DC on Monday. I will suggest to him that we go for coffee or something to discuss it, someplace intimate where we can be kind of alone, so I can bring on my powerful Vampire female charm, to emotionally beguile and mentally seduce him; I have had much practice in using them, with great success if I do say so myself.

The Voice chimes in,

Sounds to me like the makings of the basis of a decent plan.

She has what she believes is a private thought,

This is beginning to remind me of what Marlena's Ghost would do to me. She would sometimes drive me crazy.

The Voice abruptly interjects,

I heard that!

ELEVEN

Angel Returns home to Baton Rouge, Louisiana, goes first to the young girl's house to get her little dog, her pal, Bandit. As usual, she picks him up, and he vigorously starts licking her face. She pulls him away and lovingly says,

"Hey, little buddy, how many times must I be ah tellin' ya, not to be ah doin' that?"

As she gently places him down, he lets out a soft bark, and the young girl leans down to fasten his leash. As she straightens up, Angel hands her the money for taking care of him. She thanks her, and Angel leaves with Bandit walking out in front of her.

Now at her Condo, as she enters, she has the wonted impulse to shout… Gabby I'm home… stops when her memory kicks in once again that her Angelic sister is no longer here. She flops herself into the couch, and Bandit jumps up into her lap, she gently holds his ears, and for some much-needed reinforcement, she states,

"Well, my little buddy, I still has ya, Victor musta' somehow, ah reckoned, I'ds be alone someday when he gave me ya for my birthday, a while back."

With a deep sigh, she leans forward, gently puts the dog down on the floor, rises, and heads to the Kitchen to have a meal while entering her latest case into her journal in her laptop computer. With her food in the microwave, she starts up her laptop and activates the word program to update her mission records. With her fingers on the keys, she takes a moment to contemplate just how to enter this extraordinary case that she dealt with in Paris, France. She starts to type, then abruptly stops… remembering how Gabby would be so excited to hear about her latest mission, how it went, and also be very happy that I was back home safe once again. With these woeful thoughts of Gabby, a single tear rolls down her cheek. Looking up toward the heavens, she sorrowfully laments out loud,

"Gabrielle, my sweet, beautiful, innocent, angelic sister, you may be gone from this here place, but I shall never forget ya, and we will be together again, one of these days! And likes I vowed to you that night, when you was expirin', while I was ah holding ya in my arms. I dun took real good care of, that author person Harkness, that monster, that did this to you, and me. She has been ah terminated for good and all."

After eating and updating her mission records, she closes the laptop, and her Cellphone rings. She sees that it's Victor and answers,

"Hello, my lover man, what might I be ah doing for ya?"

"Well, my beautiful Angel, I'm ah real glad to be ah hearin' your voice, I'm ah calling you to find out how it went for ya in Paris. Yawl is at home now. I was ah figura it?"

"Yup, I's ah home, ya figured it right, and it was a very strange case, but I took care of it fir em. I do believes that their case is now closed."

"Good! Any other assignments goin' on fir ya, right now?"

"Not that I ah knows of, but I do needs to gets myself to DC for a debriefin' soon."

"Ah… so, maybe when you are here we…."

She cuts him off,

"Victor, my love, we shall be a seeings bout that when I be ah getins there. Okay?"

"Yup, you bet, just let me know when you's is ah coming."

She lets out a soft sexy giggle, then questionably implies,

"Don't I always?"

"Now, my love, that was ah mite suggestive!"

She replies,

"I knows it!"

Then takes the phone away from her ear, and laughs robustly, and thinks,

I sure did; need that.

Suddenly there is a soft knocking on Victors' Office door.

"Excuse me, Angel, someone's at my door."

"Yes, Victor, by all means."

He puts his Cellphone down on the desk and calls out,

"Yes, come in."

The receptionist, Meghan, slowly opens the door just enough to poke her head in, responding by informing him,

"Mr. Vincent, Sir, you has a call on line two."

"Please, tell em to hold on, and I'll be with them soon."

"Sure will do, Mr. Vincent, Sir."

He picks up his phone to tell Angel,

"I am so very sorry fir that, my love. It was the Office receptionist Meghan to tells' me; I have a call."

"So kay, sweety, I reckon we can talk later, you best take the call, and ya can call me back when you get finished with ah doin' your business call."

"I will; shouldn't belong. Talk soon."

They both hang up.

So he presses the blinking line-two button on his desk phone and lifts the receiver,

"Hello, Mr. Victor Vincent speakin', whom mite I have the pleasure of addressin'?"

"Well, Sir, you do not know me, I am an archaeology grad student, and recently, a fellow student of mine informed me that a Skull with the fangs like a Vampire was unearthed recently in Eastern Europe. I know and understand you are the Curator at the Smithsonian of historical and ancient artifacts department. I just thought you might be interested in something like this."

"Oh, yes, I am that, and ah, quite interested, are ya here in DC?"

"Unfortunately, I'm not at the moment, I'm in New York City, but I could be there in DC, on this coming Monday, late morning."

"That'll do for me just fine, and excuse me, my dear, by the way, might I be askin', ya name."

"Oh my yes, I am so sorry. Where's my manners? I haven't introduced myself, have I? I am Rachael Valli, of Terrytown, New York."

"Okay, so you can call this Office when ya gets here in DC, on Monday, and we can most likely meet somewhere for lunch. Now, how's that sound to ya?"

"That sounds just great to me, Mr. Vincent! Talk to you and see you then. Bye."

"Okay, so long."

He reflects,

A Skull with what looks like Vampire fangs? Very interesting. I have heard of this but never seen one. Maybe she has pictures, and if there was going to be one found, it makes sense it would be in Eastern Europe.

"Now, to be ah callin' my Angel back."

Angels phone rings,

"Hello, darlin'. Yawl, finished there, with your business call already, now?"

"Yup, it was a quick one, no big deal. So when yawl think you be ah comin' here, to DC?"

"Possibly, I would reckon on this here comin' Wednesday."

"Great! I'll be gettin' all I be needin' to cook your favorite meal, at the little place they have for me when I'm here, in DC. It's always so grand to be ah seein' ya!"

"Victor, darlin' ya just ah saw me last week."

"I knows that, but is ah seeming' likes a whole month ago! So, I reckon ya will call me to tell me when ya will be ah gettin' here."

"Yawl reckon right! See ya then. Bye."

"Yup, bye, my love."

TWELVE

Rachael Waits In the Plaza Hotel lounge for Lucy to show. She is getting a little impatient, so she picks up her phone to call her. As she begins to find the number on her speed dial before she can press it, she looks up, and at that very moment, Lucy shows up at the entrance archway to the lounge, looking around for her. Rachael notices that Lucy is standing there looking around to see where Rachael could be in the room, so Rachael stands up and waves her over to where she is seated. Lucy catches her doing so and then walks to the table and sits. Rachael remarks,

"Hey girl, for a minute there, I thought you weren't going to show."

"Well, I'd say you were wrong about that because here I am. So, where is the wait-person? I could use a cold drink! All the cabs were taken, so I walked. It is a few blocks."

"And you did some window shopping on the way. Right?"

"Did happen to see some nice things on my walk here, I'd love to get, but money is a little tight for me right now, starting some new classes, and that means new reference books to buy."

"That's cool. But there is no wait-person; you need to order at the bar. What do you want? I'll get it for you!"

"Okay, but I'm not a big tipper!"

"Yeah, I know that. Now, what will it be?"

"A White Wine Spritzer, please!"

"Coming right up!"

Rachael returns with the drinks, and they continue their conversation.

"This is a nice place. May I ask how you can afford this?"

"Well, don't you remember my inheritance, I didn't leave it behind, and then there are royalties from the book, which I get electronic deposits under my author name of Mia Harkness."

"Oh, that's awesome, so that is the pen name you've been living under!"

"Hey, girl, if Mark Twain could do it, so can I!"

"Mark… Um, was that the kid that sat beside you in English class in school?"

"No, silly, Mark Twain, you know his real name was Samual Clemens, he wrote all those, Tom Sawyer novels, and other stuff using a pen name, and he lived under that name."

"Oh, Yeah, Right! He lived his whole life under his pen name?"

"Yup, most of it, for his early writings at least!"

"Yeah, okay, so cool. Anyway, you are going back to Sleepy Hollow soon?"

"Not right away; I need to go down to Washington, DC, have ta check on my Copyright registration of the Book first, then I'll head back."

"Is it nice up there?"

"Yes, very. And no, there isn't a Headless Horseman Riding around chopping off heads, actually there never really was one!"

"But, I thought…."

"Lucy, please, my poor sweet, gullible girlfriend, it was just a famous fictional story."

"So maybe on a break, I can come up there to see you sometime?"

"Well, maybe, but I am there in the disguise of Mia Harknesses' look-alike cousin Rachael Valli, now, so if I am still there when you want to come to see me, you would need to play along with my little innocent deception."

"Wait, what do you mean by still there?"

"Well, Lucy, I am living in the Riverside Bed and Breakfast. It is a lovely place on a road that runs along the Hudson River. But if my money runs out or gets low, I would need to leave."

Lucy looks at her watch and states,

"Well, if you need to relocate, you will please inform me, and speaking of leaving, I need to go! I'm supposed to meet with Danny at the New York City Library very soon now."

"Danny? What happened to Jason?"

"Long story, have ta tell you about it some other time! Sorry."

With that, she gets up to go, saying,

"Thanks, Rach, for the drink. It has been awesome seeing you!"

Rachael stands up, and they hug with a mutual kiss on the cheek.

"Awesome to see you too, bye, for now, Lucy!"

Now with Lucy departed, Rachael sits back down and has some sorrowful thoughts,

And maybe forever my good friend, if for nothing else, then to keep you safe from my insidious Vampire facet, inherited from my birth father: Michael Valli.

She finishes her drink, pays her bar tab, and leaves for the stores to buy what she will need, for when she meets with, Mr. Victor Vincent on Monday for lunch.

She puts the new light blue skirt suit away from her shopping and the briefcase that fits her laptop in it. Later she will type up a phony document to be the one that was sent to her by this fake fellow student, in which she will give the phony name of; Paul Stanford.

And then search the internet for whatever else she could use to spark his interest in the Skull Artacfact, but mostly get him interested in her.

Her search of the internet for a skull with the fangs of what looks to be a Vampire; produces very little information. Still, she does find a paper from some years ago, with the notion of the possibility of one being found someday, in Eastern Europe, so she copies it to her computer, then alters some of the text a little so that this document is somewhat, brought up to date, enough to be germane for her intentions, and to acquire this man's intimate attentions. Hoping to beguile him enough so that he loses interest in this Vampire Skull probability, so as to turn his focus on me, musing,

Then, I will have him in my powerful Vampire influences, to win him over to have my way with him, and then do a turning on him into something like me, the kind of thing this U.S. Marshal hunts down to bring to justice or their destruction.

She then irately slams her fist on the room desk, stands up, and ferociously proclaims out loud,

"Hence, I shall have my revenge, on this woman, this Angel Seraph, this, this U.S. Marshal, Special Agent, for hunting me, and endeavoring to destroy me!"

THIRTEEN

Rachael Arrives In Washington DC at about eleven-thirty on Monday morning, parks her car in the visitor's lot of the Smithsonian, dials the number for Mr. Vincents' Office, the Institution's receptionist, Megan answers,

"Smithsonian Institution, good morning. How may I direct your call?"

"I'd like to speak to Mr. Victor Vincent if you please."

"And who, may I say, is calling?"

"He is expecting my call. I am Racheal Valli."

"Please hold on; I'll see if he's available right now."

"Yes, of course, thank you."

She waits on hold for about one minute. Then suddenly she hears.

"Hello, Ms. Valli, I'm really sorry to be makin' ya wait; I was on another call."

"That's okay; I'm here in the parking lot. What now, Sir?"

"First, you need to stop addressing me as, Sir! Please, just call me Victor, that'll do just fine. Okay?"

"Yes, sure, and you just please call me Rachael."

"Okay, Rachael, good, now that we have the formalities outa' the way. It's a little cloudy but still, a lovely day, leave your car there in the lot, I will come out, meet me at the bottom of the front steps, and we can walk to The Capital Grille restaurant for lunch, it is close to us at 601 Pennsylvania Avenue, it's a nice pleasant walk."

"That sounds just lovely; okay, see you soon."

As she exits her car and walks to the stairs, she thinks,

He sounds very nice and very accommodating. This just might be easier than I thought it would be.

As they leisurely walk along closely together to the restaurant, their hands every so slightly grazes up against each other, a few times; when this happens, Victor gets a slight warming sensation from her momentary touch, he brings his hand up to see why there is nothing to see. He does not know or could ever suspect that she has started her seduction of him; she knows she is close to a need for a Blood Passion feeding, so her Blood is heating up, which can be felt by touching her almost anywhere on her body. So he just shakes it off, as her having very warm hands, and does not give it another thought.

As they enter the restaurant, Hostess Maggie addresses him,

"Ah, good afternoon, Mr. Vincent Sir., very nice to have you back with us once again; your table is waiting, right this way, please."

He moves aside to let Rachael follow Maggie to their table first. Once seated, their wait-person approaches to greet them and introduce himself; he stands behind Maggie as she hands them both a menu wishing them,

"Please do, enjoy your lunch!"

They reply simultaneously,

"Thank you; I'm sure we will."

She then quickly goes back to her station at the entrance door podium.

"Good afternoon, and welcome to the Capital Grill. My name is James. I will be your server today. May I get you something from the bar?"

Victor lowers his menu to give Rachael a questioning look.

She replies to James,

"Oh, yes, I will have a glass of Red Wine, please."

James then turns his attention to Victor, inquiring,

"And you, Sir?"

"Ah, yes, James, I will have myself a dry Martini. Just tell the bartender, it's fir me. They know how I like it."

James leaves to attend to their drink order. Rachael queries of him,

"It would seem to me; you frequent this place quite a bit?"

He gently places his hand on hers and begins to answer her inquiry while feeling the warmth of it again and finding its pleasure throughout his whole body. He slowly removes his hand away and sits back, taking a moment to collect himself, hoping that she did not notice his delight in touching her hand. Rachael knows what is happening to him, so she just lowers her head and smiles. She raises her head and reiterates,

"So you come here often. Do you?"

He clears his throat, picks up his napkin to wipe his sweating brow, and answers her,

"Yeah, well, um, it's close by, and the food is excellent!"

"And they do know how you like your Martini, too!"

"Yeah, there is that."

James shows up with the drink order and inquires,

"Are you two ready to order?"

Rachael answers,

"Yes, I think so. I'll have a cob salad. What is the house dressing?"

"It's a Red Wine Vinegar, made fresh to order."

"Okay, James, I'll have that."

"And you, Sir?"

"I'll have the Monte Cristo sandwich."

"Sir, is that with the mustard sauce or the maple syrup?"

"The maple syrup, please."

"Very good!"

While they have their meal, they talk, but the subject of the Skull does not seem to come up. It seems he is too much infatuated with Rachael and wants to know more about her. She has worked her beguiling Vampiric powers, just as she planned; she tells him just enough about her to keep and make him even more interested.

She then asks,

"So, do you live nearby?"

"No, my home is in Atlanta, Georgia. But the Institution recently acquired a small studio apartment nearby, for me when I'm in town for an extended time."

"I don't want to sound too forward, but might I see it if it's not too far away, that is?"

"It's not too far from here. We can get our dessert and coffee to go and have it there."

"That sounds just lovely!"

Just then, James shows up, asking them about dessert.

Victor looks at Rachael, questioningly implying,

"Tiramisu and coffee for two, and we'll take it to go, please."

Rachael agrees,

"Yummy, one of my favorites!"

In his apartment, they sit on stools in the breakfast alcove and begin to have the dessert. Victor takes one bite and slowly pushes it away, saying,

"This just ain't sweet enough fir me!"

"You could put some sugar on it. That might help. I have this girlfriend who puts sugar on frosted....

Before she can finish her statement, Victor leans into her, attempting to steal a kiss. She immediately but sensually places her hand on the back of his neck and pulls him in for an extremely intense embrace. Their hands start to go all over each other's bodies. In unison, they move off the stools heading to the front of the room and somewhat clumsily move towards the bed, undressing each other as they move awkwardly to fall together gently into his bed entangled in an intense embrace. Their encounter is fast and furious. They both attain bliss rather quickly, gently rolling away from each other. Victor softly utters,

"Wow, I reckon that there was surely an intense thing!"

Rachael leans up on her elbows and replies,

"I do believe Sir., your slight southern accent is coming out."

"Yup, I have a Georgia accent, it's not so intense as a Gulf Coast one, but it's there."

He slowly rises from the bed and heads to the Bathroom.

Rachael lies there thinking,

I have him, now to take my claws out and get in deeper with my fangs. I just need now to get the sleeping pills I brought with me into his coffee. While he's fast asleep, I will seduce him with my Blood, gently taking some from his neck and then cautiously, but slowly injecting it back into him. He will awake with a heightened appetite for Blood; then I really have him. Now, that was easy enough. This Angel woman of his can't be much of a lover.

Victor comes from the Bathroom, feeling rather thirsty, so he goes over to the counter to drink some of the tainted coffee. He sits in a comfortable chair and states,

"I really don't know where that came from. It feels like I should apologize to you for being so intensely aroused by you. It was very," Victor's words break off as he yawns, "ungentlemanly like. Excuse me, please, suddenly I'm feeling very fatigued."

She pats the part of the bed beside her saying,

"Come, lay down with me, and get some rest."

He lays down, and just before he passes out, he softly mutters,

"I just don't know what came over me. I really should get back to work."

Then he closes his eyes and quickly falls off to sleep.

Rachael hears the strange voice in her head, for what she hopes is her last time.

Now it is my time to be resurrected, I, 'Malice the First'… shall live once again!

FOURTEEN

Victor Finds Himself in what seems to be a strange state of a total black abyss. Far off in the distance, he can see two red points of light that appear to be getting slowly closer to him. To him, it occurs. They are floating toward him in mid-air and getting larger as they do this. Then he hears a strange, eerie echoing voice declaring,

I will be within you. We will become one, co-exist, and be unique in all the world, yours and mine.

Hearing these words, he abruptly awakens. As his eyes snap open, he sits straight up, sodden with sweat and breathing heavily. Lying awake next to him, Rachael reaches up to gently place her hand on his shoulder. Feeling her touch produces a calming effect for him, so his breathing slows to normal. She soothingly requests of him,

"Please, Victor, my love, lay back down and be calm, be not afraid. What is happening to you is a good thing."

He turns his face to her's and is slightly startled to see that her eyes have turned red. He stammeringly observes,

"Yur… your eyes, they're ah… red!"

Then she smiles, which shows him her fangs, he starts to move away from her, she takes hold of his shoulder, keeping him from getting away, saying,

"Victor, please, you need me, and I need you, and we will soon need each other."

"But the voice, it...."

She tenderly places her hand over his mouth and calmly assures him,

"It, my love, I mean he, will give you power beyond what you could right now possibly perceive. In time you will understand and submit to something that can make you immortal."

She gently moves his face away from her to be able to access his neck, for a second of three transfusions is needed now, he is powerless to stop her, the slight discomfort of her bite melts quickly, into energizing pleasure, he closes his eyes, and his vision is awash in a red swirling mist. Also, he's experiencing the sensation of being in a wildly rapid spinning, seductive Cyclone.

Victor falls back to sleep after Rachael did the second taking of his Blood, and then it was injected back into him by using her fangs. It is all part of the turning. His sleep was dreamless this time. He awoke somewhat rested, but his neck was sore, and he had a thirst for Wine. Knowing that he would, Rachael had poured him a glass and left it on the night table on his side of the bed. He drank it down like it was the last glass of Wine on Earth. He attempted to rise from the bed but felt a little dizzy, so he just sat on the edge. Rachael takes the empty glass from him and asked,

"Would you like some more?"

"No thanks, what I'd like is to know just what is going on here. What have you done to me, and why?"

"Those are not easy questions for me to answer."

"Yeah, but I'd still like to know, so I suppose the Skull thing was just a ruse to get to me. And for land sakes, why me?"

"That's a good question, and I'd have to admit, you do deserve an answer. You were having a romantic relationship with someone by the name of Angel Seraph, right?"

"Not were, I am!"

"Well, you will find it nearly impossible now."

"Rachael, please, what in the world are you talkin' bout?"

"Okay, so hold on to yourself, because in approximately two days from today, you will be a living Vampire, needing to ingest the Blood of living beings about every two weeks to stay alive, just like I am and my father was."

"Wait just a doggone minute here, hold on here a second, you're ah tellin' me that you are a living Vampire and your father was, what about your mother?"

"Okay, here," as she pours him and gives him the Wine, "you have another glass of Wine, and I will tell you the whole horrid story."

When she finishes telling him the whole grotesque and complex account of her family, as best she can, his initial reaction is,

"So your father, this man, Michael Valli, is dead?"

"Yup!"

"And how do you know about Angel and me?"

"Believe it or not, she tried to kill me, back in New York City a while ago, because that is what she does for the U.S. Marshal's department, she hunts down the supernatural things, and beings, in this world, it is her job, it's all she does. Didn't you know that?"

"Well, I do know she worked for the Marshals, but not exactly what she was doin'; she only told me she handled classified special cases for them. Wow, this is mind bogglin'!"

"And, here's something else, you just might find crazy and quite unbelievable, is that I don't think she is of this Earth."

"Wait, you think she's what, an alien or somethin'? Come on, what could make you think that?"

Rachael laughs,

"Well, Victor, I do have good reason to. But, we can discuss that later."

"Yeah, okay, but Rachael, I'd still really would, like to know the reason why you have done this to me?"

"Well, it started out as an act of revenge on Angel, but now having met you and having been intimate with you, I do believe I've developed some kind of feelings for you and was so lonely, you just can't imagine what it is like to be, the only one of my kind in this, whole wide world, also before you feel you need to ask, there is no stopping what is happening to you."

"Okay, but what, or who is the voice in my head?"

"You do remember in the story, there was a, what my dad described as, a mutated Vampire Bat, that attacked him? And then existed in his psyche, well, I thought like my mom did, that it was destroyed when my dad was, but it was not because it somehow made its way into my Godmother Marlena. Still, when she was also destroyed, my mom and I just figured it was finally gone for good, but we were wrong, I'd guess. I just recently found out that it has been lying dormant inside my psyche, regenerating itself, replenishing its strength, just waiting for a new host to conjoin with, and now it would seem, it will transfer itself into you, almost like it did to my father."

"So, Rachael, what, can ya tell me, will this symbiotic being thing do to me?"

"According to my dad's memoirs, it won't do anything bad to you. It will do things to help you survive. And don't ask me how it came to be, or where it came from, that's something even my father didn't know because if he had, I'm pretty sure he would have put it in his memoir, and there is no mention of it."

"Well, I reckon I should thank you for the explanation, but surely not for what you did to me. And you say there is no way of reversing it, so in about two days from now, I'll be living like you? So what do you suggest we do now?"

"You say you have a house in Atlanta; we should take my car and go there; I can, and will help you work through this; what do you say to that?"

"I'd say it's a good idea as any, so I'll just take a leave of absence from my job, and we can go."

"Just like that, Victor?"

"Yup, you truly haven't given me much of ah choice, Rachael."

"I'd guess not! So pack up any things you need, and let's get going."

FIFTEEN

Rachael And Victor drive south to Atlanta.
Rachael breaks the sterile silence,
"So, Victor, how are you doing? You're awfully quiet. Are you okay? Victor!"
He opens his eyes, looks over at her driving, answering,
"I am okay, I reckon. I'm just very thirsty for some Red Wine, is all,"
"I'm sorry that I disturbed you sleeping."
"Reckon, I dozed off for a bit. It seems I'm still a mite tired."
Rachael explains,
"That's because of your loss of Blood. On its own, it does take a while to replenish, so as soon as we get to your place. I will give you some of my Blood. It should help. You should be able to extend your eye teeth fangs after you get some more sleep and one more transfusion, which I will do for you. After that, the transformation should be far enough along by then for you to be able to have a full Blood Passion feeding."
"Ah, one more transfusion?"
"Yup."
He questions,
"Blood Passion feeding?"

"Remember I told you about it in the Memoir? That is what my dad called it."

"Oh yeah, right! I remember now, I'm ah still reelin', from all this."

"You'll be fine. It takes a little time, is all. And like I told you, I'll help you through it. Now that is something my father did not have, someone to help him deal with what was happening to him; he was on his own."

"Oh, it must have been like a nightmare for him!"

"Well, I wasn't there, so all I know about it is what's in his Memoir, and I've read it several times."

"You still have it?"

"It's in a desk drawer in my room, where I live in Sleepy Hollow. It's actually all I have of him, kind of precious to me."

"I would reckon so!"

Victor's Cellphone again begins to vibrate in his pocket. He takes it out to see that there are a few text messages from Angel and declares,

"Oh, man, I completely forgot!"

"You forgot what?"

"Angel is comin' to DC on Wednesday for a debriefing on the assignment she had in Paris, France!"

"France! She went to France for her work?"

"Yup, and I went with her, but I came back early before she finished."

"So why come to DC for her... you know?"

"Because the U.S. Marshals' central Office of operations is in the Supreme Court Building, right near to the Smithsonian. And anytime she comes here, we usually get...."

Rachael quickly puts her hand up in a stop motion and announces,

"Victor, please stop right there! Don't need to know anymore!"

"Yup, okay, but what are we, ah goin' to do?"

"Well, we... I mean, you are not going to be in DC!"

"She's gonna' wonder where I am."

"Your Office will just tell her you're on a leave of absence."

"So when she's finished with the debriefing, she will come to Atlanta looking for me."

"Yeah, so she won't see your car there. She will see mine; I will answer the door, and just tell her that you're having me house sit while you'd be away, problem solved!"

"I just hope that works. Angel can be relentless when she wants to find someone. I know her she won't give up that easy, I… I just know she won't."

"Victor, please, you're getting all worked up. You're going to blow a fuse, so do not text her back. Just close your eyes and relax."

"Yeah, yeah, okay, take the first cut-off you come to, to Atlanta, then stop, and set your G.P.S. for my house at thirty Cedar Ridge Rd. It's the last house at the end of the road."

Rachael has somewhat disturbing abrupt thoughts,

Wow, that address and the house location seem similar; actually, it's very close to mine back in Mystic, Connecticut. It just might be a little serendipity.

So, before Victor falls back to sleep, he hands her the keys to the house. Her G.P.S. leads her right to the house, and what a house it is. It's two stories and looks to her to have maybe nearby sixteen rooms on about three acres of land. She pulls her car up the driveway, parks, and then checks her Cellphone for any messages or missed calls, in which she has neither. Victor begins to wake, so she softly says to him,

"Hey, Victor, we're here, Victor, come on, let's get you inside, and I'll take care of you after I get you into bed."

He slowly sits up, sluggishly opens the car door, and gets out at the same time Rachael does. She goes around to his side and aids him into the house's back door. Now inside, he sits on the couch and breathes a deep sigh of fatigue. She brings him a large glass of Red Wine and sits down next to him, asking,

"You must make some good money at the job you do."

"No, not really, this here house, although I live in it, and have fir awhile, it does not actually belong to me."

"How's that?"

"I'm an heir to the Vincent Textiles Corporation. Have you ever heard of them? You may not have, but much of the clothing that you buy and wear, the materials it takes to produce them is from my families' company."

"No, but on the way here, I did notice some billboards with the ads for that company."

"Well, my Granddaddy started up the company back in the forties, and it grew into a multi-million dollar business, in which my daddy and brother run the corporation now. I just get a monthly allotment and this here house to live in for free."

"Nice, my dad lived in a nice large house too, that he was given by his Grandfather, and I lived in it for a while myself, before I left it for reasons, I'll tell you about sometime when we get you all fixed up. Okay, now drink the Wine, and get up to bed. You could use some more rest before we need to continue with your new way of living."

Victor wakes up mid-afternoon of the next day, having slept for about sixteen hours. He slowly makes his way to the Bathroom and then downstairs to the Kitchen, where Rachael is sitting at the table with her laptop open checking, her E-Mail, and things.

A sizeable, wooded area surrounds this large house, with a large lake at the back of the property. So she had gone out during the night hunting to satisfy somewhat her need for Blood from the animals that inhabit the area, very similar to what she did as a young girl when living at her home; the last house on Pine Place, in Mystic, Connecticut. Rising from her chair, she closes the computer and approaches Victor, and says,

"Victor, open your mouth so I can have a look at your eye teeth. Ah, yes, one more of my Blood injections, and they should be ready to extend, for the exchanging of our Blood to make the turning complete."

"Is it very uncomfortable when they extend?"

"The first time a little, but you get used to it, and then it's no problem at all because you will also have very fast healing powers. One of the strangest things is that your eye color turns red just before and during the Blood Passion feedings, and you can see at night like its day time, then they go back to, ah yeah, let me see, ah yes for you, blue. And you will also have increased physical strength. But, you do already know some of this."

"Daytime, sunlight, that's what I wanted to ask you about. What's the deal with that?"

"Well, too much direct sunlight isn't really good for anyone, Vampire or not, but for me… us, it's slightly more intense, so overcast days and shaded places are okay."

"Oh yeah, the eye color changing thing; it was really weird when I saw yours do it."

"Well, you only saw a minor change because, in the daylight, you won't get the night vision part of it, so the red coloring will not be so intense. It's a lot to deal with at first, but you'll get it after a while, and there will be more powers and an understanding of your conditions of existing the more you feed."

"More powers?"

"Yup, you'll see in time. Malice and I will assist you with them!"

"Malice is?"

"A Symbiotic Lifeforce, from where, not really sure, but it will not harm you, it will most of the time, be helpful for you and itself to thrive."

"Weird!"

Rachael giggles,

"Yup, a little at first! But unlike my father, I, and most likely my Godmother, Marlena, we didn't have, what you do have, me to help you cope and understand it all. But I do believe she had my father's spirit, helping her along a little."

"Wait! Your father's spirit!"

She giggles again,

"Don't you believe in Ghosts?"

"Well, I do believe I need some more Wine and more sleep."

SIXTEEN

Angel Parks Her custom made black and purple Harley Davidson Motorcycle in the parking lot section, designated for the U.S. Marshals at the Supreme Court Building in Washington, DC, to promptly attend her meeting with Director Hughes for her debriefing of the 'Nightstalker' case that she was sent over to assist on, in Paris France. This meeting takes about an hour and ends a little after noontime. She is invited to have lunch with the Director but politely declines the invite, saying that she needs to go to the Smithsonian to see her beau, Victor. The Director completely understands and wishes her well, adding that he will be in touch with her soon if any new cases arise. She answers in the positive and leaves.

Leaving her Bike where she parked it, she walks to the Smithsonian that is relatively close by, entering the circular room that is, the reception area for multiple Offices, one of which is Victors. She approaches the receptionist Megan, looking busy at the desk, and is recognized. Megan looks up and politely addresses her,

"Why, Agent Seraph, it's a pleasure. What might I do for ya?"

"Well, It's Megan, right?

Megan nods, yes.

"Okay then, Megan, is Victor in his Office?"

"Don't you know?"

Slightly perturbed, Angel answers her,

"Don't I know what, missy?"

"That Mr. Vincent has taken a sudden leave of absence. We all believe it just might be a personal, family medical thing."

"Is that what yawl reckons?"

"Yup, I mean, yes."

"Did he go home to Atlanta?"

"I don't know where he went. He sure didn't tell me. I was informed yesterday in a memo on my computer about him taking a leave of absence. I'm sorry, but that is all I know."

Megan lowers her head to go back to what she was doing before Angel came in.

Angel walks over to Victors' Office glass door with his name, Victor M. Vincent. In the eloquent lettering on the glass, she looks inside but sees nothing advantageous, she tries the door, but of course, it is locked. As she passes by Megan's desk to leave, she says,

"Well, thanks, yawl, have yaself a nice day now."

"Yup... yes, you too!"

As she begins her walk to where her Harley is parked, she thinks,

Leave of absence? Why would he take a leave of absence and not somehow let me know? He knew I was coming. Something is crazy here. I'm goin' to havta' drive down to Atlanta and see if he is there.

As she walks by the Smithsonian parking lot, she takes notice that Victor's company car is still parked there, in his assigned space. She walks into the parking lot to look inside his vehicle. Doing so, she has a thought,

Why would he not take the car?

She looks inside the car but, seeing nothing of any consequence. Lightly placing her fist on the roof of the vehicle, with her other hand on the locked door handle, she softly inquisitorially thinks out loud,

"Victor, my love, what in heaven's name is ah goin' on here, this ain't like the man I know and love, at all? I really must go to Atlanta."

She quickly gets her Bike from the Superior Court Parking lot, pulls out, and heads south for Victors' house in Atlanta, Georgia.

While in the Kitchen on her Laptop, Rachael hears what she believes is a Harley Davidson Motorcycle pull up, and stop at the front of the house, so she goes to a front window to see, and sure enough, she recognizes Angel's unique custom design Harley Davidson Motorcycle, she then goes upstairs to find that Victor is still asleep, and thinks as she goes back downstairs,

Good, I'll handle this myself and get rid of her. Although I'd like to kill her right here and now, that wouldn't be an act of satisfying revenge, better she will have to eventually hunt the man she loves to his death or destruction, which will kill her slowly in a way I never could.

As she steps onto the floor at the bottom of the staircase, the doorbell rings. Not responding to the bell vocally, she goes to the door, slightly opening it, leaving the chain on, so as not to show her whole face, and acting rather meek and mild, she inquires,

"Hello, what is it?"

"Well, I's is ah lookin' for the man that lives here."

"He's ain't here, I'm house-sitting for him while he is away, and before you ask, no, I do not knows where, he went, or, is, or why, so I'd appreciate it, iffin you'd be on ya way, now!"

"Okay, but might I be ah knowing your name?"

"Oh, sure, but I don't knows what good it will do yawl. My name is… um, it's Linda, Linda Masters!"

With that said, she closes the door.

Angel saunters to her Bike and once more tries to call Victors' Cellphone. It goes right to his voice mail. She just hangs up without leaving a message. She mounts her Bike and rides away into town to get something to eat.

After watching Angel drive down the road and out of sight, she goes up to Victor's bedroom to do, while he is still asleep, what should be the last extraction of some of his Blood into her, letting it mix with hers, then injecting it back into him, it should and will give him the ability for his fangs to extend for his first time, so he can have a Blood-feeding, with doing that his transformation will be very close to complete, she then announces aloud,

"Malice should then be able to join with him mentally and gain the strength he... it will need to be whole again and conjoin with a Human host once more. I can feel him... leaving me the more I give Victor my Blood and ever so slowly infiltrating Victor's mind and body. I am only the catalyst for Malice to be regenerated and active again. I just wonder if any of my truly biological, late father, Michael Valli, is still within Malice.

Back once again, now sitting in the Kitchen, Rachael has thoughts of what should be the last of the instructions on finishing the transformation of Victor into the new, no the next Malice.

When Victor wakes soon and feels strong enough to have his first real feeding, I will go out into the wooded area and get a good size animal of some kind to have his initial Blood Passion feeding. After that occurs, he and Malice should be close to being completely merged within one mind and body, just like my father and Malice were. To have even a small amount of my father in my life would be truly amazing!

SEVENTEEN

Angel Stops For some supper at Hattie B's Hot Chicken restaurant, she has just finished her meal when her Cellphone rings, quickly she pulls it from her pocket, hoping it would be Victor, finally calling her, but to her disappointment, the caller ID shows it to be her boss, Director Hughes of the U.S. Marshal's Department calling, she answers,

"Good evening Sir. What might I be ah doin' for ya?"

"First, I need to know. Where you are?"

"I am in Atlanta, Georgia just havin' some supper afor I heads back home."

"Good, Angel, can you stay there tonight? I was hoping you could meet with the Atlanta area Game Warden in the morning, something about some animal being found in a wooded area, dead with no Blood left in them. So, can you please handle this one for me?"

"I reckon so; I've nothing else, ah doin' right now."

"Great! I'll E-mail you the details in a while, and thanks, you truly are an Angel!"

She has a quick thought,

You don't know how close you are to the truth. But even for you, it has to remain a secret.

She books herself into a nearby Motel and gets settled in for the night. She opens her laptop to read her E-mails, but the one from the Director has not come through yet. She lays back on the bed, looking up at the ceiling, and sorrowfully laments,

"Victor, oh my sweet lover Victor, where can ya be and want's ah goin' on with ya? I do very much wish ya woulds call me."

Her verbal thoughts of Victor are interrupted by her laptop sounding off, telling her that a new E-mail has just come through. She sits up to open and read the message. It is the one from Director Hughes, giving her the details of the meeting with the Atlanta area Game Warden Office tomorrow morning. After giving it a quick read, she lays back and softly whispers,

"Victor."

Then lets out a deep sigh and falls off to sleep.

In the morning, after she has her breakfast, she re-checks the details of the E-mail from the Director. And goes over it in her mind,

So, at ten AM at the Atlanta area, Game Wardens Office, I am to meet with Officer Sarah Burns. Okay, good, I sure could use the distraction right now.

After a cordial impromptu quick introduction meeting and a brief explanation from Officer Sarah Burns, she drives them both to the edge of the forest, parks the car on the road, and they enter into the deep woods where a Deer was discovered about a day ago by a hiker.

As they walk through these dense woods, on a trail pre-marked out by the Officer, they eventually come to a small clearing and come upon the medium-sized Deers' rotting carcass, which looks oddly partially flattened. Also, it's quite apparent that its neck looks to be broken. Likewise, they can plainly see that there are two small puncher wounds on its neck, blackened now with its dried Blood.

Angel walks around the animal, getting as close to it as she can stand, because the stench and the many flies buzzing around are quite a disgusting hindrance. She makes the um sound a few times as she is inspecting the scene. She looks over at Officer Burns, who is standing with her head down about ten or so feet away from the dead Deer, and informs her,

"Well, as you already knows I ain't no Veterinarian, but I do reckon, and you just might find this ah bit hard to believes but, this here animal was attacked, and killed, by a Vampire."

Officer Burns tightens up, lifts and shakes her head, and responds,

"What!... Wait!... Did you just say... a Vam... Vampire? There just ain't no sucha' thing as...."

Angel quickly closes the space between them, gently places her hands on the Officer's shoulders, interrupting her, and explains,

"Officer Burns, I knowes' how crazy it might be ah soundin' to yawl, but believes me there is thins' in this here world, ya will finds, very hard to be ah believin', but let me tells ya, there is thins' out there, that would makes ya hair turn white! I knows, I's has seen em, and have dealt with em, it's why I do this here job, dealin' with thins' like this, it's my Specialty, hance my official title: U.S. Marshal, Special Agent, Angel Seraph."

"So, Marshal, what are we to do now?"

"You should get some pictures, afir this thin' is utterly decomposed. You will need a good and believable cover story, or yous is ah gonna' has a panic on your hands, and yous needs to keep people out of these here woods, afir you dids has yaselfs a murder of a person, or a whole bunch of em"!

Officer Burns takes several photos with her Cellphone, all the time muttering softly,

"This is just too... much too unbelievable, a Vampire right here... a Vampire in Georgia... here in Georgia!"

Angel tries to console her by saying,

"Officer Burns, Sarah, you just ah can't go to pieces on this here thin', yawl needs' ta ease your mind, and start ah thinkin' clear, yawl gonna' needs' a real good cover story to release to the press."

As they get back to the car, Officer Burns stops before opening the driver's door and declares,

"I got it!"

Angel stops before she gets in the car to see what she has to say, so replies,

"What does ya got, girl?"

"Gators! Yup, Gators out in the woods, we can put out a notice that Alligators have been spotted prowling out in the woods. After all, there is some in the large lake nearby."

"Well, that just might be ah keepin' the common folk out! But what about the Hunters?"

"The Hunters has themselves firearms."

"Oh, yup, good up again,' Gators, but not, up again' Vampires!"

Officer Burns asks,

"Guns won't take down a Vampire?"

Angel's explaining answer is,

"Not by usin' regular bullets, they will slow em' down, a bit, but not kill em.'"

"Then what should be used?"

"Silver ones has ah more powerful effect, on em'."

"Okay, then them there Hunters is on their own."

The car pulls into the Office building parking lot and over to where Angel's Bike is parked. Just as Angel begins to exit the vehicle, Burns announces,

"That sure is one sweet ride yous got there. Custom job. Right?"

"Yup, she sure is! Cost me plenty!"

"I'll bet. So thanks for what you could do here. We sure do appreciate it."

Angel exits the car, begins to then suddenly stops, walking toward her Bike, quickly turns round takes a small pad from her breast pocket, writes down her cell number, leans in the passenger side car window rips out the page, with her number written on it, and declares,

"Sarah, I'll be here tonight, come mornin' I'll be a fixin' on leavin' for home, so here's my cell number just in case somethin' else comes up, related to the 'V' thins,' whilst I'm a still around these here parts."

"Okay, thanks, but I just hopes we won't, has to be ah botherin' ya anymore, then we has already."

Angel mounts her Bike and slowly pulls out of the parking lot, thinking,

Mite just be, ah maybe, I should hang round her a little longer, I has me some strange feelings about what happened to that Deer.

She then throttles up, disappearing down the road out of sight, back to her Motel room, to make contact with her Boss, Director Hughes, to give him an update.

EIGHTEEN

While Rachael Is enjoying her morning glass of Wine, she suddenly hears Victor let out a thunderous manic yell from the upstairs Bathroom. She puts her glass down on the living room Coffee table, almost spilling it, and runs up to see the matter. She knocks on the closed Bathroom door only to hear Victor softly moaning,

She knocks again, requesting,

"Victor, please open the door!"

"Com… come in… it's o…open!"

She opens the door slowly to find Victor on the floor with his head down and his knees up in his chest, with his arms wrapped around his legs and his head down, hiding his face from her, holding on tightly. She kneels in front of him, places her hands on his shoulders, and lovingly inquires,

"Victor, my dear, what is it, another one of those bad dreams?"

He answers her,

"No, it's not that!" and continues with his hands covering his face. As he lifts his face to hers, he takes his hands away and declares,

"Look! This is how I looked in the mirror a minute ago", then he continues, "Oh dear lord! Look at me, just look at ME! I look hideous!"

"Victor, you look okay, you look quite normal, now, please get up and have a look for yourself. You look like your handsome self."

He stands up to have a look and is pleased to see that he does look normal. He feels his face and says,

"I… I was getting ready to shave, I bent down to get my thinks out from under the sink, and when I came up, my eyes were red, and my fangs were out over my bottom lip. I looked loathsome, like some kind of a monster! I… I…"

Rachael turns him around, and after wiping a small amount of Blood from his chin from when his fangs protruded, gives him a comforting hug and says,

"Victor, my sweet, listen to me, please. I know, the first time you see yourself like that can be a bit of a shock, but you will get used to it, and besides, you don't normally see yourself. Your victims do, and it is the last thing that they will ever see, as my dad wrote in his memoir, the first time you see him… Malice, that is, is the last time you see him. You, um, we only see a red haze in our vision, telling us that our eyes have turned red, signaling that a Blood Passion feeding is needed and near. It is a shocking sight for your victim, providing both you and me, that is, the element of surprise which causes them to freeze momentarily. It can even work on animals. Which is what you need to have, rather soon, I'd guess."

With Victor composed now, they make their way downstairs to the living room to sit on the couch and continue the conversation. Rachael picks up her Wine glass from where she left it, on the Coffee table, but before she takes a drink from it, she asks of him,

"Victor, would you like a glass?"

"Yes, I could use one, but wait, so, your dad called the Vampire side of himself, Malice?"

"Yes, like he wrote in his memoir."

"Do you have a name for your Vampire side?"

"Yes, I do, but until recently, I didn't have a voice in my head, as my dad did, and you do, and will, but I gave it a name regardless."

"Oh, yeah, what name did you give it?"

"Well, with all due respect and reverence to my late father, I chose… Malevolence,"

Okay, now let me get you that Wine."

She rises and goes to the Kitchen.

Victor responds loud enough so she can hear him,

"That's sort of a female version of Malice. Right?"

She returns, hands him his glass, and explains,

"Just like my name, Rachael is the female version of my late father's name, which, as you now know, was Michael."

Victor surprisingly answers,

"I did not know that, about those names, I always thought…!"

She quickly interrupts him to finish his thoughts,

"That the female version of Michael would be Michelle, you are not alone. Most people think that, but they, like you, are wrong. Just think of the spellings of my name, Rachael, and my dad's name, Michael; they are very similar to each other."

Victor finishes his Wine, places the empty glass on the Coffee table, leans back, and yawns.

"Victor, you really need to get some more rest, because after your first full Blood Passion feeding, in which I will go out later to get you a good-sized animal to have it, then I believe Malice will fully conjoin with you, and it could be a little rough, so please get some sleep, and do not be too worried about it, I will be with you to help you, all I can."

With that said, Victor rises from the couch and slowly makes his way upstairs. Rachael takes the Wine glasses to the Kitchen. Looking out the window, she takes note that the sun is getting low and thinks,

It's much too early for me to go out, to hunt down another Deer, this time for Victor to complete his transformation. I will wait for it to get dark and then go out.

Out in the backyard, Rachael sits in the dark, in one of the lawn chairs, with her head down. She puts her hands over her face and concentrates for a while. When she lifts her head and takes her hands away, her eye color has become red, so she can now see like it is daylight. Also, her fangs and fingernails have extended, along with her other Vampire powers. She has once again, at will, manifested… Malevolence! Rising from the chair, she sniffs the air, turns herself in all directions; until she detects in what direction she can smell an animal's fresh Blood coursing through the body of a good size Deer. In doing so, she heads out into the forest in that direction. Moving stealthfully and downwind of her prey, she observes a Deer taking their last drink of water for the night from a small stream. Very slowly and quietly, she gets in a position that will enable her to spring upon it, taking it down quickly. She easily gets it to the ground with her heightened strength and knocks it out with her fist. She will need it still alive when Victor takes its Blood when she gets it back to the house.

As she is carrying the unconscious animal over her shoulders, unfortunately, she had not noticed that her knockout punch opened its skin, and its Blood is very so slowly dripping out from its wound. As she walks along, she can hear, more like since, that something is gradually pursuing her, not footsteps. Something like a scraping type sound, as if something is dragging itself along the ground, she stops walking, quickly turns round to find that an Alligator is following right behind her, letting the Deer drop to the ground behind her, putting herself between the Deer, and the Gator, it has also now stopped, so as quickly as she can, before it can open its mouth and lunge at her. She, using one foot, stomps on its head, crushing its skull, it lets out its last long breath, and it dies.

She picks up the still unconscious Deer, turns round to look down at the now-dead Gator, and has a thought,

Grotesque, hideous monster, you picked the wrong prey tonight.

Then continues on her walk back to the house.

NINETEEN

Rachael Waits In the Kitchen after she had helped Victor out in the backyard, gets started on having his first full Blood Passion feeding, consuming the Blood of the Deer she brought for him. She continues, from earlier, looking through a local newspaper that was delivered to the house, finding a small article of some interest to her; it's a report of a Deer being found in the woods that the authorities claim was killed by an Alligator foraging for food, it goes on to warn people to stay out of the forest until they sound the all-clear. She irately puts the paper down, with questionable thoughts,

Now, why didn't I get rid of that Deer by throwing it in the lake? Dumb, girl, really dumb, not to cover my tracks, once again getting too cocky, and oh sure, now they tell me, about the Gators in the woods, that was probably the Deer, I killed for my, Blood Passion feeding a few days ago. But they're not entirely wrong; the Gators are out there; I myself had that encounter with one just tonight, unlucky for it. Well, that probably means that the authorities just might be poking around the area soon; it kinda reminds me of what happened to me back at the Cliff House in Mystic. This place is getting to be a little too coincidental for my liking. I just might need to relocate us, sort of like I did, when I faked my death and left the Cliff House in Mystic and ended up living in Sleepy Hollow using a new appearance and the alias name Mia Harkness. And Sleepy

Hollow just could be the place for us to go to; after all, I still do have my room there.

After a while, Victor comes in the back door, into the Kitchen, somewhat shaken, and Rachael helps him to a chair. She asks of him,

"Victor, are you feeling okay?"

He slowly raises his head and replies,

"I… I think so; that was amazing, the rush of power. Now I see what you meant. Is it like that every time? It is quite exhilarating!"

She goes to the sink to get a damp paper towel to wipe the Blood off his chin.

"You had better go up to bed; I believe Malice will become sentient of you; now that you've had your first full feeding, knowing what it could be like, you should be laying down, remember what it said in the memoir."

He raises a little unsteady, saying,

"Yes, I believe you're right."

"And Victor, to answer your question, yes, it's like that every time, every single time!"

With Victor now upstairs, she reasons,

I do need to get rid of the dead Deers' body; this time, I'll take it to the lake out in the woods and throw it in, for the Gators to feed on, that should dispose of its now empty carcass totally, so it can never be found. Malevolence, I will need my Vampire powers once again.

Standing, now out in the backyard, over the Deers' dead body, she concentrates, quickly changing into her Vampire persona, with all the powers that go with it. After reaching the lakeshore and pitching the animal carcass out into the lake, she carefully walks back through the forest, being somewhat vigilant of any potential danger that may present itself. Still, of course, with her Vampire powers activated, not much of anything could harm her. As she walks, she has memories of younger times when she dealt with the mutated Vampire Raccoon at the Cliff House in Mystic.

When she gets back to the house, after an uneventful return through the woods, she goes upstairs to check on Victor in his bedroom where he still might be in bed sleeping, without knocking;

she enters the room, it seems to her that he is asleep, she quietly approaches him to get a closer look, softly asking,

"Victor, my dear, sweet Victor, are you asleep?"

She stops and thinks,

Now, ain't that one of the dumbest questions to ask someone, the one other being, are you dead. You will never get a yes answer to either question.

Surprisingly to her, Victor's eyes pop open, by seeing that the color of them is red makes her realize that it is not Victors' consciousness, which is awake and aware. She takes a step back and enquires,

"Malice, is that you in there?"

With a guttural version of Victor's voice, he answers her,

"Yes, my dear Rachael, it is I. I am renewed, Malice, the First, or should it be the second? Could it be I could use a new name? Do you have any suggestions, my dear girl?"

"Well, off the top of my head, maybe something that would go well with Victor, as it was with my father and you: Michael and Malice, so what do you think?"

"I am not sure, so if you come up with something, you can let Victor know, and so will I. For you do know that what he will know, so do I."

She sits in the chair at Victors' desk and thinks for a moment, suddenly she gets a notion and suggests,

"Wait, how about Valice?"

It agreeably answers her,

"So then it would be Victor and Valice. Well, maybe, ah well, yes… yes, I do kind of, like it, as you Humans might say, it has a nice ring to it, Valice, the First!"

She replies,

"Well, don't know about nice, but it does sound okay to me; when Victor is awake, I shall confront him with it and see what he says."

This entity, for the time being, Valice, agrees with her and then goes eerily quiet, smiles maniacally, and then closes Victors' eyes.

Victor wakes up about an hour later. Rachael sitting in the room notices his eye color is his normal blue and says,

"Good morning. How are you feeling?"

He rubs his eyes, looks up at her, and replies,

I feel like my old self, just a little thirsty, is all."

She reaches over to the desk to get a glass of Wine she had brought up; anticipating his needs, she hands it to him, saying,

"Here you go, my love."

"Thanks, you are a sweetheart!"

"Not really. I just know what you'd want or need."

"Had a funny dream; at least I thought it was a dream."

"What do you remember of it?"

"Why don't you tell me what you can recall of it."

"It wasn't so much visual as it was audible.

"What do you mean?"

"Want I mean is, I could hear you talking to someone, that was not me, but it was me. It was bizarre."

"What is it that you remember hearing?"

"Okay, let me think. It categorically was you talking to someone with a gravelly version of my voice. Now, doesn't that sound weird to you?"

"Okay, so let me try to explain it to you in the best way I know how."

"Rachael, please do try. But before you do, has Angel shown up here yet?"

"Yes, she did, and as I told you, I told her I was your house sitter, so she left. It was no problem, so stop worrying about her. I don't believe she'll be back any time soon."

She assures him with her fingers crossed on her hidden hand.

"Okay, now, Victor, back to your dream. What do you remember being said?"

"You were talking about a name for my Vampire persona."

"Yup, I was, to you! Well, essentially, your, as you would say, Vampire persona. So what was it you heard or recall hearing."

"What I vaguely remember is you coming up with the name Valice and then putting them together, sort of a title for me."

"And that was?"

"Victor and Valice!"

"Yup, very similar to my father's title of Michael and Malice. Do you approve?"

"Yup… I mean yes… yes, I do!"

"Good, now get some more rest; there are some things we need to discuss soon."

With that, Victor closes his blue eyes and goes back to sleep

TWENTY

Angel, Arrives Back at her Motel room, calls Director Hughes to give him an updated report of the Atlanta Game Warden Officer's meeting, and requests that she'd like to stay in the area for a little while longer. He completely understands, so he tells her to do what she feels is best.

In the morning, she calls from her room the Motel reception Office to notify the person at the check-in desk that she would like to extend her room stay for a week; her request is confirmed. She heads out for breakfast at a local place. After her meal, while having her second cup of coffee, she calls the Game Warden's Office to speak with Officer Burns. She waits on hold for a moment.

"Ah, hello. Are ya still there?

"Yup, I am still here."

"Officer Burns is out on a call. Would you like me to transfer the call to her, or do you want to call back later?"

"Um, can ya tell me where she ah might be right now?"

"Well, yup, she's out at the forest where we had a crazy report of a dead deer."

"Might I be ah askin'…"

Before the person on the phone can finish, she says,

"Thanks, yawl bye!"

Angel suddenly hangs up her Cellphone, grabs her Helmet from the empty chair at her table, leaves the money for her meal with a healthy tip, goes outside, jumps on her Harley, and speeds off to that location.

As she arrives at where the Office's patrol car is parked on the road, she sees Officer Burns walk out of the woods with two men; one young and one older looks to her as possibly a father and son, perhaps. The older-looking man is dragging a sack behind him. She's not sure what to make of it. She just stands at her Bike with a puzzled look on her face.

Officer Burns notices her and proclaims with delight, "Marshal Seraph, I was just about to contact you, and like magic, here you are!"

"I was ah tryin', to contact ya earlier to let ya knows; that I'd be ah stayin' round these here parts for about another week or so, there is something real peculiar goins' on around these parts, and I'd like ta investigate a mite more. Iffin yous don't mind."

"Mind? Not at all, Marshal; the more help, the merrier, as far as I'm concerned!"

"So, what yous have there, in that there gunny sag, yous is ah draggin'?"

"These here two gents found it on the lakeshore, so they called my Office, so they sent me out here to have a look-see."

"Okay, so what is it yous got there?"

"First, let me introduce yawl; gentlemen this here lady, is U.S. Marshal, Special Agent, Angel Seraph and these here two gents are; Pete Clark Sr., and Pete Clark Jr.; round here; we folks that knows em' so just calls em; Pete and re-Pete."

"Okay, now can ya gets to showin' me what yous got there in that gunny sag?"

"Oh ya sure, Marshal, we can do that; Pete, would you open it and empty out the item, please."

He unties the gunny sag and dumps it out onto the road.

Angel takes a look-see and states,

"Well, okay, looks to me like the head of a dead deer!"

"Marshal, have yaself a closer look at it, please

"Yes, Officer Sarah, I will!"

"I don't sees anythin' strange here; let me try flipping it over and has myself a closer a look-see!"

Pete Sr. hands her his hiking stick. Angel flips it over and is not very surprised by what she sees, so with no abrupt reaction. She utters to the Officer as she starts to walk away from it, not wanting to draw too much attention to what she has instantly noticed.

"Sarah, please, if you would step over here."

Officer Burns obliges her and asks,

"Sure nuff, what is it, Marshal?"

They both turn around, away from the men.

"Did ya sees em, there on its neck, them there two small puncture wounds!"

Officer Burns puts her hand over her mouth and questions in a muffled manner, so no one else can hear her,

"Vampire again?"

"Yup, sure as shootin', glad I stuck round here. That's what yous got here. Now, who is ah living about these here parts?"

"Come on, Marshal, let's go to my car and have us a look-see on the computer, at the map of this here area."

They sit in the car to see on the map that there are six residents nearby; one, of course, is Victors' house.

Pete Sr. approaches Officer Burns's car window to ask, "Officer, excuse me, but might we be ah goin' now?"

"Why yup sure, you two can leave, but I'd be wishin' that you both not be sayin' too much of what you two found out here, and I will need to confiscate it for a forensic examination. Okay?"

"Yup, sure, bye now, you has yawl a good day!"

Officer Burns turns her attention back to Angel and asks,

"What happens now?"

"Well, I needs to be getten' the Deers' head in for, like you told Pete Sr, a forensic examination."

"Where?"

"The Smithsonian in DC is where. I'll call my boss; he'll be havin' a private carrier come to transport it there and then send the results report to your Office."

"What should we do in the meantime?"

"We needs to canvas this here area, on your maps, and sees what we can be ah findin'."

"Oh, you mean like gatherin' intel?"

"Yup, Yawl got that straight, girl!"

They put the Deers' head back in the gunny sack and then place it into the Officer's car trunk, then Angel follows her back to the Atlanta Game Warden building.

Back at the Game Wardens' Office, Angel calls the US Marshals Office to make the arrangements for the item pick up and drop off at the Smithsonian and open an official investigation case file.

TWENTY-ONE

Rachael And Victor sit on the couch close together, relaxing, enjoying a glass of Wine and each other's company.

"So Victor, my darling one, how do you feel after your good night's sleep?"

"Well, Rachael, my dear, I feel someone empowered and a little strange with this voice in my head."

"That is something you will get used to and find it will be very beneficial to you."

"I'm a little curious about something."

"And just what might that be? My sweet."

"Well, I have seen what I look like in my neoteric Vampire guise; I am wondering what you look like in yours."

"You're curious, are ya? You do know what that did to the cat?"

"Yup, I heard that one from my mother once a twice."

"By the way, Vic, I have noticed that you've lost your light southern accent."

"Yup, I go to say something in my accent, but instantly my mind says it in a northern accent like you talk; weird ha?"

"No, not actually Vic; Valice, your alter ego, learned to talk, I should really say communicate, from my father and also from my Godmother; both were northern accent speaking people."

"So, what you are saying is, that when I speak, so does he, I mean 'It,' I mean… not very sure what I mean. It is all somewhat perplexing to me right now."

"Yup, I know, my father had to go through and deal with this by himself; at least you have me to help you with understanding what is happening. What was it you wanted to ask me before we when off to you being curious about something else. So what was it you wanted from me?"

"Oh ya, I was just wondering what you look like when you become your Vampire self; that is what I wanted."

"Do you really want to see me like that? You may not like what you see? As a matter of fact, I believe I know, you will not like what you see."

"Wait, you can actually bring it on at will?"

"Yup, I've been living with it for a long, long time, ever since I was seven; that is when my hunger for Blood started. But I only went after animals at the beginning; my first aspire for a Human Blood-feeding was when I was almost Twenty-one, and the opportunity presented itself to me, but I don't really want to talk about that right now."

"Well, on second thought, maybe your right. I wouldn't like to see you like that, so forget I even asked. Okay?"

"Yup, is there anything else you have the need to know about?"

"Yes, there is; I thought I heard you say something about that; we had a lot to talk about just before I fell off to sleep."

"Um, yes, I did. I want to talk to you about how you would feel about us leaving this place."

"So let us talk!"

"Not right now, my love lets go upstairs for a while; we can talk about it after we have some fun."

"Okay, let's go!"

"Yes, you grab us a new bottle of Wine, and I'll see you up there. And sweetheart, I promise I won't start without you!"

"You had better not, grrrr!"

Rachael giggles sexorily as she runs up the stairs.

After an intense measure of lovemaking, they both fall off to sleep in each others' arms.

Victor finds himself lying alone in the bedroom filled with a red mist, or is it his eyes having turned, so the room just looks to him that way. A shadow falls across him, and he looks up to see what looks to be Rachael with her red eyes and fangs hovering over him; her image starts to lean in closer to him as she opens her mouth slowly, showing her long white fangs, he cries out,

"Noooo!"

His yell wakes Rachael lying beside him; she turns to him and holds him to comfort him. Realizing he must be having a nightmare; she tries to soothe and calm him softly, saying,

"Victor, Vic, my love, wake up; you are having a bad dream!"

Hearing her voice, he wakes, breathing heavily, opening his eyes to see all looks normal, and he begins to breathe normally as he sits up; Rachael comes from behind and whispers in his ear,

"Victor, whatever it was, you're okay now; it was just a bad dream, just a bad dream."

"I'll say it was a bad dream; you were going to…

He stops mid-sentence.

"I was going to what?"

He swings his legs off the bed to sit on the edge, runs his hand through his hair, and replies,

"Nothing… nothing it was, as you said, just a bad dream. I really don't want to talk or even think about it."

"Alright, my love, we do not need to talk about it; if you do not want to."

He slowly rises from the bed to get some Wine, from his desk, pours himself a glass, and inquires,

"Rachael, sweetheart, would you like a glass?"

Still lying in bed, she answers him,

"Come here, lover; I'll have some of yours."

He hands her his glass and sits on the edge of the bed.

"Now, what was it you needed to talk to me about?"

"Okay, while you rested, I went out to get a few things, and I happen to hear some people talking, more like whispering, actually."

"Ya, so what's up with that, and why should we be concerned?"

"Well, sweety, it was what I heard them saying that has me troubled."

"And what pray tell were they saying?"

"Something about a dead deer and the head of one being found with weird marks on their necks! And I also heard someone mention about a strange woman in town riding a hopped-up Harley Davidson Motorcycle is involved, and I'm sure we both know who that could be."

"Okay, so what is it you want us to do?"

"Victor, my love, it would be to our advantage; for us to leave here soon."

"And go where sweetheart?"

"To my room at the Riverside Bed and Breakfast up in Sleepy Hollow, New York. My room is there, all paid up for the next six months or so and waiting for my return. So what do you think, my love?"

"Okay, so when should we go?"

"How about early tomorrow; that sound okay for you?"

"Yeah, but we will need to go to DC so I can turn in to them my resignation; the car I have is one of theirs, so now they can give it to my replacement."

"Yes, my sweet, I see no problem in doing that. Will it take long?"

"It will take me longer to write it out; than to just leave it and the keys to the car at my Office with reception and go!"

"Okay, good, we should pack up tonight, and then we can leave early in the morning."

"Sounds like a plan, babe!"

TWENTY-TWO

Angel Receives A call from her boss, Director Hughes requesting that she come to DC pronto for a briefing on the item she had them pick up in Atlanta.

She replies,

"Will tomorra be soon enough, Sir?"

"In the morning, please, Angel; would be just fine by me."

"Okay, by me too!"

"Good, see you then."

They both end the call.

She slides her phone into her back pocket as Officer Burns approaches, and she asks,

"Is there a problem, Marshal?"

"No, not really; they just want me ta come ta the DC Office for a briefin' tomorra mornin', and then I'll be back here with the written report, so your department can have yourselves a copy for your files."

"Okay, good for a minute there. I was ah thinkin' we ah mite be losein' yawl."

"Well, not till this here case can be closed, will I be a leavin' yawl."

"Okay, so hows about us ah getin' some suppa?"

"That here sounds a mite good to me; I's ah hungry!"

"Ribs?"

"Yawl bets!"

"Good, I knows a great place nearby, come on, and I'll drive."

"Right behind ya, girl, I means Officer!"

With a smile, they head out for the car. As they ride burns asks,

"So Marshal, do ya thinks we's has ourselves a real, honest to goodness, Vampire round here?"

"I wouldna' say goodness, but there is a good chance of it."

In the morning, with the meeting over, Angel, after she has quickly checked in at the Smithsonian to get any news about Victor; to her disappointment finding that he has turned in his resignation and left his job there, Angel proceeds to head for the ramp to get on the highway heading South back to Atlanta. Slightly earlier, Rachael and Victor, after he had swiftly run in to drop off his resignation and keys to the Smithsonian's car and Office, are getting on the opposite ramp of the same highway in DC, where they'll be heading North up to Sleepy Hollow in New York State.

As they both merge on opposite sides of the highway into traffic, they go by each other without knowing it. Victor, with his heightened senses, just for an instant, has himself a strange inkling that Angel is somewhere close by. He mentions nothing about it to Rachael; he does not feel it is relevant and does not want to distract her from her driving, he just casually looks around but sees nothing of her on the road, and besides, it's kind of hard to miss that customized Bike of hers'.

Victor stops looking around, so he settles down, leans his head back, closes his eyes, requesting of Rachael,

"So pray tell, my love, please continue."

"Yes, of course. Where was I? Oh yeah, so I ditched the car on the side of the road and made my way to the nearest town and acquired another vehicle to regain my things and continue on my getaway."

"On your way out of Connecticut to Sleepy Hollow; Right?"

"Why yes, my love, you are so perceptive."

"Well, my sweet, it was easy enough to figure out; you were almost out of the state of your home."

Rachael begins to have feelings of melancholy, saying,

"Yes, my home, but Sleepy Hollow is my home now," turning her head to him and continuing with, "and soon it will be yours!"

"Sure looks that way to me unless we will need to relocate again. It all sounds rather exciting to me. You should write a book about it someday."

"I have written a book, but not about me. I do believe I had told that to you."

"Yes, you did, and I am dying to read it."

"Please, Victor, do not forget to these people at the Inn; that I am Rachael Valli, Mia Harknesses look-alike cousin!"

"Not to worry, I will not forget that."

"There are some copies of the book in my room at the Inn. You most certainly can read it there."

Angel arrives back at the Game Wardens' Office Building in Atlanta to give Officer Burns the copy of the findings report.

As she hands it to Officer Sarah Burns, Sarah nervously questions,

"Is it what ya thought?"

"Haves' a look fir yourself."

Burns sits down and unseals the large envelope, but she looks up at Angel with an anxious expression on her face before she takes out the report.

Angel tries to give her courage by saying,

"Sarah, don't yawl be fearful; I am here to hep you people in any way that I am able ta; after all, it is my job, and I reckons I am known to do my job very well, very well indeed. Nothing and no one gets in my way of that; it is the reason I have comes down here fir."

Before Sarah looks at the report, she says,

"So it be true we haves us a real…

Angel cuts her off,

"Looks at it and lowers yur voice, please! Cuse me, I'll be right back, I be ah needins' me a ladies room break."

Angel returns to see Sarah sitting with the report in her lap; looking somewhat bewildered, she asks,

"So whats ya thinkins'?"

"It looks to be a mite indecisive to me."

"Yup, they's ain't too sure what to make of it."

"So where do we ah go from here?"

"We're ah gonna needs to wait a while and see what happens next. A good amount of this here thin's is ah waitin' game. Meantime, lets' us go canvas the neighborhood and talk with some of these here nearby the lake area residents and finds' out what we's can."

"Okay, just let me notify my boss that we'll be out for the day."

"Yup, and maybe later we's can gets us some more of them there ribs, they was mighty delicious!"

"I'm with you, Marshal!"

"Please stop with calling me Marshal; just calls me Angel."

"Alrighty!"

"Victor, wake up; we're here!"

They get their cases out of the trunk and make their way into the Inn Lobby. Mike greets them jovially,

"Good afternoon, folks!"

Rachael steps out from behind Victor to announce,

"Mike, it's me, Rachael, and I like you to meet my friend Victor who will be staying with me for a while."

Mike extends his hand cordially to Victor.

"Real nice to meet you, Sir, and it's real lovely to have Rachael back here with us once again."

TWENTY-THREE

Rachael And Victor settle into her pre-paid room at the Sleepy Hollow, Riverside Bed, and Breakfast. Victor lays on the bed to check it out. He proclaims,

"I like this bed! But don't you feel that it's a little too bright in here?"

Rachael answers him from the Bathroom while she is freshening up a little,

"Well, sweetheart, draw the shades!"

"I will, yes now that is better."

"Darling, dinner is not served until six. Are you at all hungry for food? There are many animals that live along the Hudson River just on the other side of the road if it is a quick fix of Blood you need."

"No, my dear, what I am in real need of is some Wine."

"Need or want?"

"Sort of both, actually."

"Inside the cabinet, the Television is on; however, my dear, it is the Wine from Europe I told you about, so it's quite a bit stronger than the Wines you can get here at home in America."

"I do remember you were telling me about this Wine; in my worldly travels, I have had the Wines of Europe, so I am well aware of that. Still, I do appreciate you giving me your lovingly reminder. So where is a copy of your... I mean your look-alike cousins' book?"

She wryly smiles and informs him,

"Now, that was an amusing way of putting it; there should be a few copies up on the shelf in the closet."

Now, with a full glass of Wine and a copy of the book 'Mystic Vampyres', he gets comfortable in the chair by the shaded window that overlooks the front of the Inn.

Rachael rests on the bed deep in thought,

So after he finishes reading the book, I will confront him with the possibility of us starting our own real Vampire Cabal, like in my first published novel, 'Mystic Vampyres' by me, as Mia Harkness.

About halfway through his Wine and the book, Victor asks Rachael,

"Do you have something I can use as a bookmark?"

"Yes, I have some custom-made ones from the publisher, just a minute, I'll get you one.

From the shelf in the closet where her book's copy was, she brings down a small box with some promotional giveaway items for the book, handing Victor a Bookmark, he says,

"Thanks, hun, this is a very nice bookmark, and the book ain't half bad!"

She slightly angrily proclaims,

"Half bad! What is that supposed to mean?"

"Well, don't you think that it's a little childish?"

"No! Not at all; it's supposed to be a romantic tragedy! Do you find romance stories to be childish, Victor?"

"No, not in real life but in this story, it just seems to come off that way to me; I'm sorry."

"Well, my sweet, you have not finished it yet, so you can hold your opinion until you have finished it."

"Okay, will do. How about we go for that walk around town, so you can show me off and around? It is a partly cloudy day, so we should be okay. Right?"

"Yes, that is what I promised you, didn't I. And yup, we should be just fine. By the way, you really have lost that Georgia accent for good, I think."

"I sure have, and I kind of like it."

Rachael enters into the A B Ladies Shop first, and the young girl attendant Rose, greets her cordially,

"Well, it's mighty nice to be ah seeings you again! It's Miss Rachael, right?"

"Yes, it is, Rose, and this is," as she motions to Victor to enter the shop, she continues, "As you might say, my beau, Victor!"

"Well well, It's ah mighty nice be ah meetin' ya Sir, Mr. Victor!"

"Southern girl! From… ?"

Rose and Rachael reply to him concurrently with,

"Eden, Mississippi!"

Rose comments to Rachael,

"Why my goodness Miss Rachael, yawl recollected!"

"Yes, I did! Now my dear, what you have that's new?"

"Right over here, we has some new pretties ya might be ah likein'."

After directing Rachael to the area where the newest lady's items are, she turns her attention to Victor.

"Mr. Victor Sir, as you can see, this here is mainly a Lady's shop, but iffin there was anythin' yous might be ah needin' we, sure enough, can order it for yawl."

"That's very nice of you… Rose, but I don't need anything right at this moment, but when I do, I'll be sure to let you know."

"Good, Sir, okay, please, you be sure to do that now!"

Rachael comes to the small checkout counter with a few items for Rose to ring up for her.

Then they leave the shop with polite biddings all around.

Victor spies the 'Horseman Tavern' across the way. Rachael takes notice of this and questions,

"Glass of Wine, my love?"

"How did you know that is what I'm thinking?"

"Because I'm thinking the same thing you are!"

"So come on, let's go!"

Rachael takes his outstretched hand, and they cross the road together and enter the Tavern.

They sit at a small table off in a darkened corner of the place, drinking their Wine, speaking softly.

Victor leans into her to ask,

"So is this where you would come to attain the victims of your Blood Passion?"

"Yes, please, Victor, keep your voice down; they were all traveling salespeople passing through town by train. One was at a rather fancy French restaurant up on the river road, with the same circumstance; salesperson passing through town by train."

"Wow, so an untraceable traveler, you covered your tracks rather well. But how and where did you dispose of the bodies?"

"I would get them to take a walk with me, down along the Hudson River bank, do my feeding, then slip their body into it and let the water take them away for me."

"Smart girl, real smart!"

"I learned to use a large body of water from my dad's memoirs. I still have it; I should let you give it a read."

"Now, that I would love to read!"

"Okay, yes, so when you are finished with the book, I'll give it to you to read."

"Sounds great! Rachael, you want another glass of Wine?"

"No thanks, we best get back; dinner will be served soon, and Mike's sister and business partner Chef Jeannie is an awesome cook! And by the way, it's good you were turned using my Blood because in that way, like me, you are what I would call a Hybrid Vampire and can eat meat, also some fruits, without a problem. That helps us stay in Cognito as regular Humans."

Victor adds,

"And also, we can walk in dim daylight."

"Precisely, Victor, so come on now, I'll pay the tap, and we can go."

As they walk, Rachael remembers something,

"And you need to meet Benjamin the Inn's bellboy slash all-around helper; he is a great kid and should be around when we get there."

"Benjamin, he sounds like a nice boy."

"He is, and I think he may still have a crush on my cousin, wink wink! But I think he has switched it to me, so please don't be jealous!"

Victor lets out a laugh and declares pompously,

"I... Victor Vincent be jealous of a young boy, never!"

As they advance within sight of the Inn, and can now smell the aroma of what Chef Jeannie is cooking is pleasantly wafting through the air. They look at one another, smile, then hand in hand, quicken their pace to get there promptly.

TWENTY-FOUR

Angel Rides Shotgun in Officer Burns' patrol car to the lake area neighborhood to ascertain any information about possible strange or weird happenings within the last week or so. At the first house, they get a negative result, and it goes the same at the next four in the six of the places of their investigative area.

When they pull up to the last place, Angel requests Officer Burns to let her handle this one alone. Officer Burns agrees. Angel exits the vehicle and looks over at the driveway to notice that no car is parked there, so she just writes it off that the woman she had confronted here at Victors' dwelling before is most likely out shopping or something. She rings the bell and waits a moment, then peers in each one of the elongated decorative windows on each side of the door and sees no sign of anyone. She then knocks heavily on the door and calls out,

"Victor, Victor, it's ah me, Angel. Ain't ya at home? Please come to the door. It's ah me, Angel! U.S. Marshal Angel Seraph, please oh please do be ah answerin' me."

Officer Burns observing all that is happening, comes out from the driver side door and stands at the car, turns to be looking in Angels' direction, and calls out,

"Angel, there ain't no one there; come on, let's go. I've just received a call bout some alleged unlicensed hunters down by the lake; I needs' to go check on it right away!"

"Ok, alrighty, I'm ah coming."

She walks to the car thinking,

Victor, where oh where has ya got yaself to?

Angel gets in the car as Burns says,

"Someones ya know ah livin's there? We're not so much as gettin' anywhere like this. Ain't there anythin' else we can be ah doin'?"

"Well, yup, I reckon ya could say someones I ah useta knows was ah livin' there. And ya be askin'; what else coulds we be ah doin'? well, not we, Sarah, but I has me an idea."

"What idea?"

"I'll tells' ya when I knows' more."

As they speed off toward the lake area, Officer burns replies,

"Ok, fair enough."

On the Lake Road, Burns returns to the car after talking with the two suspects to inform Angel, that is awaiting her return, that it's no more than a false alarm, so she suggests that they go eat.

Angel agrees, and as they speed off down the road. Angel comments,

"In my line ah work, I've had much too many of them there false alarms! But like yawl, I still took care ah it."

Officer Burns just smiles in silence.

After their delicious meal, Officer Burns and Angel drive back to the Game Wardens building, where Angel gets her Bike to head to her Motel room for the night. Wishing each other well, Angel tells Burns she will speak with her tomorrow.

When Angel gets back to her room, she takes a shower and starts looking for her Cellphone charger. Emptying from her rucksack comes the charger and the book 'Mystic Vampyers' by Mia Harkness. She picks it up off the bed and thinks,

Now, why am I carrying this thing around with me?

Among all the other items that came out is a half-pint-sized bottle of Wild Turkey one hundred and fifty proof southern Bourbon. After putting the book and the bottle on the floor lamp table, she gets a glass from the Bathroom, sits in the chair where the floor lamp table is, opens the Bourbon bottle, pours a full glass of it, and quickly drinks it down. She picks up the book from the table looking at it; so she thinks,

This here Harkness woman, this murdering real Vampire author that killed my beautiful sister, Gabrielle, she just cain't have anything to do with my Victor's disappearance; I mean, I destroyed her, well I believes' I did; an then left her mortally wounded to be finished by God's elements in Central Park, New York quite a while ago. She has ta be dead; she just must be!

Pouring more Bourbon into her glass then drinks that down, she continues in her thoughts,

To satisfy my curiosity, I should call her publisher and ask if this Author is planning a second novel, yup, come morning; I believes' I'll do just that.

She unsteadily rises from the chair, takes two steps, lollops onto the bed, and falls off to sleep.

Angel wakes at about nine AM, feeling slightly hungover; from the robust Bourbon she had foolishly indulged in, she gets some fruit juice from the small fridge in her room and begins to feel a little better; enough to call the book 'Mystic Vampyres' by Mia Harkness publisher. She learns to her surprise that author Harkness is at this time in Europe on an extended book signing tour also that they are not aware if she is planning on another book yet. She thanks them and ends the call and remarks irately out loud,

"She's alive! She just caint be? I left her fir dead; there ain't no way she could have survived unless she received some hep from someone or something. But why would she get hep? She was, I mean, she is an evil murdering Vampire. Unless…"

Her words trail off, and her ranting stops; she takes in a large swallow of the Bourbon from what is left in the bottle, finishing it off to try to calm herself, and begins to think rationally, declaring,

"It's lookings to me like, now I'm ah gonna needs to take me a trip up North to that there place where I first met this Author, up there in that Sleepy Hollow town. Just mights be a clue to the truth of her really bein' alive or not, up there.

After having herself a light breakfast, she calls Officer Burns to inform her, but not giving her any details; she will be out of Atlanta for a while but will be back as soon as possible. She checks out of the Motel and gets on the road headed up North.

TWENTY-FIVE

Rachael And Victor enter the lobby of the Riverside Bed and Breakfast Inn together. The door opening chime sounds off, and Mike looks up from his paperwork to take notice and greets them with,

"You people are back right on time; we have just finished doing setups in the dining room and will be doing sittings for dinner very soon now. And if I may say so, it's a special one!"

Rachael inquires,

"So, please, Mike, tell me, do. What is so special about it?"

"Well, our excellent Chef, my sister Jeannie was here very early this morning working on having Beef Wellington with her exclusive red Grape chutney garnish on our menu this evening, in honor of you, Rachael, being back with us."

"Okay, Mike, so you must put Victor and me down for a serving each!"

At that moment, Benjamin appears in the lobby from the dining room, announces to Mike,

"Alright, Boss, we're good to go in the dining room!"

Rachael right away says excitedly to Ben,

"Ben, Benjamin, you have not met my Victor yet!"

Ben looking down at the floor, somewhat sadly replies,

"No, Rachael, I have not."

"Well then, please come say hello to him."

Ben slowly walks up to Victor with his hand out; looks up at him, and states,

"It's a real pleasure to meet you, Sir."

As they cordially shake hands, Victor replies,

"The pleasure is all mine, I'm sure, young man, and please, my name is Victor, not Sir."

"Yes, Sir… I mean Victor, and please just call me Ben, anytime."

"Sure will do, Ben anytime!"

With that, they all laugh.

Mike chimes in,

"If you would like to use the lobby restrooms to get cleaned up for your dinner, please feel free to do so. And I'll go into the Kitchen to put in your orders for the special."

"Please, Mike, let me do it!"

"Okay, Ben, go ahead!"

Ben smiles and quits the lobby for the Kitchen.

While Rachael and Victor go to the separate restrooms to clean up for dinner.

After having their delicious special dinner and meeting Chef Jeannie over coffee and dessert, Rachael and Victor retire to their room for the night. As they walk to the room, Victor remarks,

"Well, that certainly was an excellent meal; I think I'll do some more reading of the book before bed; by the way, Ben seems like a nice boy."

"He is a very nice kid and can be rather helpful at times, Victor; I just want to check a few things on the internet, and then I'll join you for bed, and if you're in the mood, we could… if you like."

"I just might like that we could thing, with you anytime!"

Victor finishes the book, closes it, and remarks,

"Well, all in all, it's not bad once you read the whole thing! I do believe there are some between the lines type stuff in it."

Rachael inquires,

"What exactly do you mean by between the lines stuff?"

"Well, the stuff about a Vampire Cabal. Is that just wishful thinking on your part, or would you like to have something like that exist?" he continues his analysis, "And the way you spell Vampire with a 'Y' instead of an 'I' seems to me to be somewhat unique."

"Yup, I wanted the cover to stand out to create some curiosity."

"Now tell me the girl Mia in this story; I know you wrote it under the name Mia Harkness, an alias or Pen name, as they are somewhat the same thing, I believe. Is she supposed to be you?"

"No, not really, just a fictitious version of me, the Author, Mia Harkness, in a different reality," Rachael comes over, sits beside him on the bed, and continues, "So what do you actually think of a Vampire Cabal becoming a real thing?"

He places his arm around her waist, looks deeply into her eyes, and states,

"So you think because your dad, who was a living Vampire, with your mom, being a regular Human, having you, a living Vampire hybrid, that we could do something like that? But I'm, by the way, I'm still trying to wrap my head around it all."

"Yup! But a whole bunch of times!"

"I'd said, Rachael, we'd have to get busy with it real soon."

She moves into his neck and starts kissing him, saying,

"Like now... tonight?"

Gently moving her away from him, he stands up, where she lays back on the bed, giving him that come-on look.

Suddenly there comes a light knocking on their room door.

Victor looks at his watch to note that it's eight-thirty in the evening.

Rachael stands up, shifting her clothing.

He leans over to Rachael, that is now standing next to him, whispering,

"You have any idea who this might be?"

"I could take an educated guess!"

"And your guess would be?"

Before she can answer him, another knock a little harder, accompanied by an announcing from the visitor,

"Rachael, Victor, it's me, Benjamin. Are you guys up?"

"Well, my guess would have been right."

Victor moves to the door; without opening it, he asks,

"Ben, my boy, what is it?"

"I was just wondering…."

Victor interrupts him by opening the door saying,

"You are just wondering what?"

Ben standing in the threshold, replies,

"Oh, yeah, just wondering if you people would like or want anything from the Kitchen; it will be closing for the night in about thirty minutes."

Victor looks over to Rachael, asking,

"You, hun, want anything?"

"I don't think so, but wait. well, not from the Kitchen, but we could use a couple of extra pillows, please?"

"Sure, coming right up! Back in a flash!"

Victor asks of Rachael,

"Should I tip him?"

"That is totally up to you, hun."

Ben returns promptly with the requested items.

Victor takes the pillows from him; there are goodnight wishes all around as he closes the door.

TWENTY-SIX

Angel Pulls Her customized Black and Purple Harley Davidson Motorcycle off of the Northbound Highway Ninety-Five in Badham, South Carolina, to get a quick meal at the Waffle House Restaurant. As she parks in the lot, everyone inside that is able to view the parking lot out of the front windows can't help take notice of her and her Bikes' unique appearance; they curiously watch as she makes her way to the restaurant door. Jeff, one of their Chefs, in recognition of Angel, gladly greets her,

"Hey there, woman, it's mighty nice to be seein' yawl again! Bean a while, whats' yawl doin' round these here parts; yah on a case or somethin'? I ams' just sapposin' yous must be hungry. So just what is it I can be gettins' fir yawl?"

"Well, Chef Jeffery, Sir, headed to a case, woulds' love me some of them there delicious Pork Chops ya makes is always the perfect choice fir me."

"Well then, woman yawl gets' yourself a seat, and I'll be ah havein' em ready fir yawl, lickety-split! Apple sauce and corn wit em'?"

"Yes, Sir, and plenty of thems' woulds' be real fine by me!"

After enjoying her meal of Pork Chops and the fixings, she orders dessert. While having her dessert; of a wedge of sweet Peach Pie with a strong cup of coffee, her Cellphone, she has placed on the table, begins to vibrate, looking to see what the caller ID shows; that it's from, the U.S. Marshals Director Offices', she frowns at this, and just lets it vibrate and go to voicemail, continuing to enjoy her Pie, she, really not wanting to answer the call right now. The wait-person shows up with her bill, places it down next to Angels' phone that she notices vibrating, and remarks,

"Cuse me, mam, but I thinks' that someone ah wants yawl on yur phone!"

She puts down her coffee cup and quips,

"Ya thinks! Does' ya? Well, just mights' be that I don't wants to be ah answerin' it just now, I'll calls' em' back after I finishes this here right sweet tastin' Peach Pie, I's is very much enjoyins.'"

The wait-person carefully response,

"Yup, as ya please, Marshal!"

While enjoying another cup of coffee, Angel reluctantly decides to return the call from the U.S. Marshals Directors' Offices.

"Good day, Director Hughes' Office. How may I help you?"

"Ah ya, this here is Special Agent, Angel Seraph returnin' the Directors' earlier call ta me, that I had missed, iffin yah please, might yah be connectin' me to him, I'd be much obligein' to yawl."

"Okay, please hold."

After a short hold, she hears.

"Hello, Angel! Thanks for getting back to us! I believe it was my Assistant Director Joseph Thurmond at my desk, using my phone that wanted to speak with you, Angel; please hold on; I'll have them connect you to him. I do believe he's in his Office now."

After about a minute wait, she is connected to the Assistant Director Joseph Thurmonds' Office.

"Hello, Angel, so glad ya called back?"

"Yup, was ah driving when ya call afore. Yous' ah fixin' ta speak wit me, Sir?"'

"Yes, Angel, I have something we need you to look into in upper state New York. Where might ya be right now?"

"I'm in South Carolina headed North for some private business to takes' care ah; I just stopped for some early lunch here at the Waffle House Restaurant. So what is it yous be ah havin' fir me up there?"

"Well, we received a call from a Captain Vivian Cates of the Bridgeport, New York Police Department about some strange going ons, up there, asking if we could send someone to help them out. And right off, I thought of you. So, would yah please, go see what it's all about? They were vague with any details."

"Yup, I do reckon I can be there early this here evenin'. That's ah, right near that there city of Syracuse. Right?"

"I just checked it on the map, and you're right; I'll call the Captain there and tell her you're on your way."

"Alrighty then, be ah talkin' to yah after I takes care of it."

Angel finishes her coffee, pays her bill with a healthy tip, gives her thanks to Chef Jeffery and all the staff, takes her leave of the Waffle House Restaurant, mounts her Bike, heads for the highway, once there she merges onto Highway Route Ninety-Five, resuming her trip Northbound.

After her six-hour high-speed drive to upper state New York. She parks her Harley in front of the Bridgeport Police station, she walks in, and Desk Sargent, Officer Jones takes immediate notice of her requesting,

"Hello miss, what can I do for ya?"

Presenting her badge, she responds,

"Howdy, Officer, I'm U.S. Marshal Special Agent Angel Seraph; I do believes' your Captin' is ah waitin' on me."

Jones picks up the house phone to notify Captain Cates that her appointment person has arrived.

He hangs up and announces,

"Okay, she will see you right now Marshal, her Office is down the hall, third door on the right."

She walks away saying,

"Thanks, Officer, much obliged to yawl."

She knocks on the Captain's Office door and hears from within,

"Please come right in, Marshal!"

She enters and is requested to have a seat. In doing so, she inquires,

"So Captin' Cates, what seems to be ah troubling yawl up here in these here parts?"

"Well, Marshal Seraph, first may I say, thanks for coming. What we have, are some strange people over in our lovely Oneida Lake area. Some of the residents around there and some of our townspeople are disturbed and, may I say, a little frightened of them. Maybe you could see what they are up to and get them out of there for us? They are residing in an old abandoned Church, I am told in the reports from my people. I have not been out there myself, so one of my Officers that ordinarily patrols that area can give you the exact location when you are ready to go have yourself a look."

"I will have me a look-see just what theys' a-doin', afta I gets' me some supper, and then gets the location from your Officer that diligently covers that there area. So can ya tells me where I can gets' me some good grub here in yur town?"

"I sure can; we have a nice place to eat called the Bridgeport Diner right downtown, so if you go there, I'll have one of my Officers, Officer Stevens; she is one of my people that regularly patrols the Lake region. I will have her meet with you at the diner to inform you of the details of this problem of ours. Okay?"

"Yup thats' be just fine with me! and I'll be gettins' back to ya, afta I be ah takein' care of yur little problem ya guts' yourselves here."

"That sounds great; you be well and safe now, you enjoy your meal at the Diner, Marshal, and it will be our treat of the Department; I'll give them a call to let them know you are coming and to charge; your meal to us."

"Sure nuff will, Captin' so long fir now, an thanks' yawl for supper!"

Angel rises, smiles and quits the Captains' Office.

TWENTY-SEVEN

Victor Stealthfully Moves along the Hudson River Bank, hunting for what is a good size animal.

He is in need of a Blood feeding, so his eyes are red, and his fangs are extended; his strength and agility are almost enhanced to about ten times that of an average person. It being a new Moon night, it is quite dark, but to his red Vampire eyes, he sees as if it were daytime; he slowly and quietly strides, with the ease of the Snake, that would slither unseen and unheard along the ground through the foliage, absent are his footsteps making any sound at all.

He sniffs at the air in the hope of finding his prey, familiar with the scent of a Deer's Blood, and he detects one to be nearby; even quieter now, he moves along the Riverbank to get closer to his quarry's location. This adult Deer comes into view, where it is between two small bushes taking a drink from the River. Slowly and very vigilantly, he flanks it to quietly pounce and overpower it to get his very much-needed Blood feeding.

The subdued eerie gravelly voice of his alter ego Valice suddenly becomes avowed and emerges soothingly into his mind,

'You have fast become rather good at this hunting for animal prey; soon, you will need to take in the Blood of a Human, which will complete your transformation, and we can be of excellent service to one another. I have co-existed within the consciousness of both the male and female

of your world's Human race. I have learned and do realize the vast differences between them; it is good to be once again within a male, for in my former existence, I was known in your world as a male of my species. I had to vacate the female Marlena's subconsciousness before her body had expired from Rachael's defensive attack, which destroyed her physical body, silently relocating my symbiotic persona, promptly implanting it vastly deep within Rachael's subconscious, without her knowledge, of course. Unknown to her, only observing her maturing into a woman, waiting for someone like you to come into her life. Although, from time to time, I have ever so subtly injected my influence into her thoughts. Growing impatient, I recently made my existence within her known to her.'

Victors' response is only a very acknowledging but lax agreeable restrained murmur,

"Mmmmm."

Now, perceiving his opportunity, he swiftly attacks the Deer, taking it down and without a sound from it, rapidly acquiring all of its Blood within him, then silently disposing of the carcass into the River, to which the rapid current takes it away for him.

Shifting and brushing away from his clothing any debris that may have attached itself to him, he takes some water from the River to clean any Blood from around his mouth or on his hands. Now looking justly presentable, he starts walking back to the Inn.

Feeling very satisfied with himself, and is now very much rejuvenated from the feelings of weakness that were coming on, which he believes had kept private from Rachael. Hearing his alter ego Valice, in his mind, strangely gave him some confidence to carry out his deed, which he did very efficiently and without any remorse.

Victor enters the Riverside Bed And Breakfast Inn, Lobby, greeting Mike at his prominent position behind the registration Desk, very energetically,

"Hey, Mike, how's it going tonight?"

"Well, Victor, despite the need to do the almost endless paperwork, it's going okay; I would have to say, the place is full up right now, and we have reservations for the whole season."

"You, Mike, and your sister, Jeannie, who incidentally is a fantastic Chef, you two do have a nice place here, with a great location, and you know what they say about location? So it sounds and looks to me like your doing much better than just, okay!"

"Yeah, I know; location location location!"

"Well, it's true, Mike, very true. I've had many friends start what was to be a great business venture, and because of the wrong location, it failed."

Mike responds, motioning around the Lobby, with his eyes and hand,

"Yup, it's a great little place; still, it's a lot of work!"

"I agree, but with employees like young Ben, I'm sure it makes it a little easier."

"Benjamin ya, he's a great kid, do need to keep him inline sometimes, though."

"Well, he's still a young boy. Is he your or your sister's kid?"

"No, an old friend of mine's, Grandson, lives two streets over. He came in one Spring day after school looking for work, so I put him to work after school and on the weekends; it's also his Summer job. He has been here ever since that day."

"That sounds real nice; as I said, you have a great little place here. I guess I'll go see what Rachael is up to."

"Okay then, Victor, you have a nice rest of the night."

"You too, my man, good night!"

Victor enters their room to find Rachael posed provocatively on the bed adorned in her; new black silk camisole that she had bought at the A B Ladies shop the other day when shopping there with Victor. She asks,

"You feeling better now, my love? Because you look better, you were looking a little pale. But you appear to have some good color now!"

"Yes, sweetheart, so you did notice, but I'm feeling okay now."

"Yes, of course, I did. I know what it looks like when a time of feeding is upon someone like us. Okay, so are you feeling good enough now to do with me what I told you I wanted a try?"

"Um, you mean the conceiving of a child or two?"

"Yes, I really thought you were in agreement about trying, and if so, we can begin trying tonight!"

He declares as he gets into bed beside her,

"Well, I'm not against trying! Still, we have done this thing before."

"Yes, we have, but not with the intentions we have now."

"Does that make much of a difference?"

"Not in the feeling of it, only in the intentions of it!"

TWENTY-EIGHT

Angel Sits At a corner table in the Bridgeport Diner, having a cup of coffee just waiting for Officer Stevens to show up for their pre-arranged meeting, her order of Fried Chicken and Waffles has been noted by her wait-person Lynn, and will be prepared when she tells them to get it cooked for her.

Officer Stevens enters the Diner, stops just inside the door, looks around, not knowing what Angel looks like, but was told she rides a Black and Purple custom Harley, which she did take note of in the Diner's parking area, now notices a woman in Black and Purple riding Leathers, with a Black full-face Bike Helmet with a striking Purple wing design on it, hanging on the empty chair back. Hence, she presumes this to be the U.S. Marshal, Special Agent, Angel Seraph, that she is supposed to meet up with. She walks over, and before she can say anything, Angel looks up at her and announces,

"It's mighty nice to meet yawl, Officer Stevens," she gestures to the empty seat opposite her and continues, "Please, Officer has yourself ah sit-down," then politely motions to Lynn to come over to her table.

"I does knows me that sound of a Harley Twin Vee Engine, no matter how quiet yous makes it. I heards ah Police issue Harley pull up outside just before yah come in and then first off took me ah notice of yur made-to-fit boots, and ah course, yur Bike Officer uniform type is a dead giveaway; so I'd reckons yawl rides yourself a Police Hog."

"Yes, it's the Police issue type. And I would imagine that is your real sweet custom job outside!"

"Yup, she sure is, and she cost me ah plenty; still; I loves her; she is my one an only partna'!"

"Well, my Captain informed me that you are here to help us with those strange people squatting out by Lake Oneida in the old abandoned Church building. I mean, there really are some peculiar things going on out there. Did my Captain happen to tell you that some of our young people from around here have been reported missing?"

"Nah… she did ant mention anythin', about missin' peoples, of any age group, ta me!"

"So, Marshal, just what is it you want or need from me?"

"First, can I be ah havin' the wait-person get you anythin', Officer Stev…?"

"Please, Marshal, call me Stella, or just Stel will do fine."

"Stella?"

"Yup, my mother named me after one of her favorite actors, Stella Stevens! Not that I even look close to what she did or does; I do believe she is still alive but a much older woman now than when my mother named me after her."

"I ain't too much familiar with that person."

"No biggy!" Stella looks up at Lynn, the wait-person, and requests,

"Just a cup of coffee for me, please, Lynn."

"Coming right up, Officer Stel," Lynn looks at Angel and asks,

"Would you want us to start cooking your order yet?"

"No, yawl had best be ah waitin' on that fir me; I needs to go with Officer Stevens and check something out. So I'll come on back to have it then."

"No problem, Miss, I'll tell the cook to put a hold on your order till you come back."

"Thanks yah Lynn, I'll be ah seeins' yawl when I gets back."

"We better take my Police Harley Marshal; it's relatively quiet for some co-vert re-con because we will need to be sort of quiet; we don't want a spook them. Right?"

"Right, okay then, yawl has yur coffee, Stella, then we'd best be ah goin'."

Lynn returns with the coffee carafe and an empty cup for Officer Stevens, fills the empty cup, and tops off Angel's cup.

They sit for a while, having their coffees, to talk a little more.

Angel explains,

"So we goes by there tonight sos' I can see where it is, and then tomorra' I'll go back, ta get me the lay of the land in the light of day, I'll be ah needins' me a place to stay just fir maybe two nights. What you guts round here, where I can gets me a room at?"

"I have a guest Bedroom at my place that my brother uses when he's around, but he's out of town on a month work detail right now, so you are welcome to use it. It would be my pleasure to have you stay at my place."

"That sounds right nice of yah, Okay I'll stay at yur place for tonight and might be one more night. I'm much obliged to yah for the hospitality."

"No prob, you're very welcome. Shall we get going now?"

Angel finishes the last of her coffee, emptying the cup, and they both stand to go; even though her meal will be on the Bridgeport Police Department tab, Angel leaves Lynn a tip for the service she has recently rendered to them, reminds them that she will be back soon to have her meal.

After they do their co-vert nocturnal re-con ride of the Oneida Lake area where the old abandoned Church building is, so that Angel can learn of its whereabouts and the lay of the land, they head back to the Diner. Stella gives Angel her spare house key and her place's address, informs her that it is the Bedroom at the back of the House, then rides off to finish her night shift. Angel enters the Diner to have her evening meal.

Sitting at the Kitchen table at Officer Stella Stevenses' place being too wired to sleep, with all her thoughts of Victor and the assumption that the Vampire Mia Harkness just might be still alive, has her mind working overtime, slowly enjoying a to-go cup of coffee she bought at the Bridgeport Diner after having her evening meal. She hears the front door open, and Officer Stevens enters, relieving herself of her Police gear then finally entering the Kitchen to find Angel in her silent deep thoughts.

Stella breaks the silence,

"Good evening, Marshal. I figured you'd be asleep by now."

"Yup, I should be, but just too wired to fall asleep right now, my minds' too full ah' thins' to rest."

"Well, I don't believe that coffee will help you sleep."

"Um, caffeine never has kept me from sleepin."

"That's a good thing because tomorrow night, you may just need all your strength and wits about you to take on just what might be residing in that old Church! There have been some talk, rumors, and believes in our little town about something Evil going on there."

"That's not whats' gut me preoccupied, takein' down Evil thins' is my specialty. I'm ah mindful with my private life's goins' ons is all. And I can't let it distract me from my task at hand."

"One of the first things we are taught at the Police Academy was not to be distracted while on duty, especially in a crisis situation; your mind must be focused on the, as you say, task at hand."

"That there is ah real good first lesson very much like, the one at the Marshals' trainins.'"

"Well, Angel, I need to get some sleep, so I'll say good night and perhaps see you in the morning. I take it you found the back Bedroom, no problem?"

"Just walked straight through to the back, and there it was; we has places like these here down South, we calls' em ah Shotgun House."

"Shotgun House, that sounds kinda cute; good night, Marshal!"

"Yup, good night, Officer."

TWENTY-NINE

Rachael sits at the desk in the room with her laptop Computer open, just gazing at the blank screen. While sipping her glass of Wine.

Victor rouses rolls over, opens his eyes to discover Rachael looking rather forlorn, sitting at the desk just staring at the blank Computer screen. He queries,

"Rach, you Ok?"

"Yup, just thinking."

"Thinking about what, sweetheart?"

"Oh, a few things such as… um."

"Such as what, Rachael?"

"Victor, darling, many things!"

"Ok, I'll bite. How much? Many things are you thinking about?"

"Lots!"

"Rachael Valli, now you're just being evasive; you know by now that you can tell and talk to me about anything that may be in or on your mind."

"I really thought that getting back to being my real self would make me feel right again… Still…."

"Yeah, still. What?"

"Well, sweetheart, there are some things I miss about being Mia Harkness!"

"Such as?"

"Being an Author for one."

"But you are… the Author Mia Harkness!"

"Victor, you know it, and I surely know it, but no one else knows it."

Declaring that, she puts her glass down and lowers her head.

Victor gets out of bed, adorns himself with his robe, walks over to stand behind her, gently placing his hands on her shoulders. Kisses her on the top of her head and empathetically inquires,

"My love, do you truly want to go back to being Mia Harkness? I mean, there is at least one person that believes her to be dead!"

She moves her hand up to touch his hand on her shoulder, replying,

"Like your ex-Angel Seraph. However, my love, there are more people, like the whole of Mystic, Connecticut, who believe that Rachael Valli is dead!"

"Still, there are those that know that she is not."

Like, Lucy and my old lover Shane now know that Rachael is alive and well. Furthermore, Shane knows that I am a Vampire, and maybe even Lucy thinks that also."

"Rach, do you think they will tell anyone what they know?"

"Perhaps, but who is there for them to tell, and would anyone they do tell, believe them?"

Victor pours himself a glass of Wine and tops off Rachaels' glass. Then he sits down next to her at the desk, adoringly covering her hand with his.

"Are you trying to say that it is easier for you to be Mia Harkness than to be who you actually are?"

"No, not at all! What I'm saying is…."

Suddenly there comes a knock at their room door. Victor rises and moves to it and inquires, through the door,

"Who is it?"

"Victor, it's me, Ben. Good morning!"

From the closed door, the conversation continues.

"What do you want? My boy."

"Just wondering if you and Rachael would like anything from the Kitchen? I am headed there now."

Rachael can hear Ben, so Victor turns to her with a look of asking if she wants anything; she responds in the negative by shaking her head no, Victor answers Ben saying,"

"Ben, my boy, we will be down for breakfast soon. Still, thanks just the same."

"Okay, see you downstairs later."

Victor sets back down with Rachael to continue with their discussion.

"Okay, were where we? Oh yeah, you were going to elaborate."

"Victor, my love, I just feel a little bored, is all. I liked writing, and I just can't think of a way to continue doing it."

"Let me give it some thought, hun, and get back to you on it.

"There is something I was wondering about that has to do with us reproducing."

Rachael puts her hand on Victors' this time to comfort him before speaking,

"So what is it you are wondering, my man?"

"I have not yet had a Blood feeding from a Human. Don't you think I need to do that before procreating someone like our kind and start? What was it you called it?"

"Victor, oh sweet man of mine, a Cabal, but you just could be right about that; remember, after all, this part of it is all new to me. I'm not so sure it will work the way I want or would like it to. So there may be plenty of trial and error. But I do think we should hold off expecting conception until you have your first Human Blood feeding. And that will be soon, I hope."

"Yes, indeed, Rachael, my love, but we can still practice. Right?"

"By all means, my love, we should continue with what we have been doing; besides, there is a lot of fun in just trying. True?"

Victor concurs,

"Extremely true, my love!"

With that said, they both stand, kiss and Rachael, lets out a naughty giggle, and they begin to get dressed to go down to breakfast.

While they sat and enjoyed their breakfast, Victor suddenly gets an idea about how Rachael could do some more writing, speaking softly; he begins,

"Rach sweetie, are you familiar with Edgar Rice Burroughs, the Author?"

"Yes, he was the creator and writer of Tarzan."

"Yup, mainly, but he did write a bunch of other things, such as a Series about a man he called John Carter in his 'Barsoom Series.'"

"Wasn't there a movie made of that a while ago? So Victor, just what exactly are you getting at?"

"Yes, there was a movie; what I'm getting at, my love, is that he created and wrote the Novels from the Memoirs of John Carter; that in a mysterious unexplained way he received and then did the writing of the series of Novels from them.

She gives him a puzzled look and inquiringly remarks,

"Yeah, so?"

"So Rach, and please, this is just my thoughts on this; you could write as Mia and just say that she is sending it to you in E-Mails."

"Now that could perhaps work, I suppose. I'll give it some thought; thanks, sweetie."

"Although my dear, if Mia Harkness has another Book Published and Angel finds out about it, she will assume that Harkness is still alive and most likely after what you had told me you did to her angelic sister, Gabrielle, she will come gunning for her, I mean you."

"Well, if you remember, my dear, she has never seen me as Rachael Valli. She does not know that Mia and I are one in the same person."

"True! But she's not stupid, remember I do know her pretty well, and also remember she did find you in New York City."

"Yup, she had to have tracked me down by using my Publishers online signing schedule, and she would try that way again, I'm sure. So, I just won't do any signings this time, so her finding me, I mean us, would be rather difficult for her, I would have to surmise! And also, by that time, you, my love, will be a fully functioning Vampire with all the powers that goes with it. She would be up against the two of us, not just me this time."

"True again! Still…"

Rachael finishes her coffee, puts the cup down then asks,

"Are you having doubtful thoughts that you just might have a problem going up against her with me?"

"Well…"

"Oh, Victor, we just may need to slay her, if she should find us, and let me inform you of something, I do remember her sisters' Blood was quite sweet, by the taste of a small amount that will very often get on your tongue during a feeding, and had given me a tremendous power fulfillment as I had never felt before. I would not mind feeling that once more, of which I now do believe most likely helped with me to be able to survive her deadly attack that night in Central Park, of New York City."

With that said, Victor lowers his head, finishes his meal, and they stand to leave the Dining room quietly.

THIRTY

Angel, Sits ON her customized Harley Davidson Motorcycle with her Helmet in her lap after making a comprehensive check of her weapons and equipment. Officer Stevens, dressed only in her sleeping attire and robe, still wearing her slippers, comes outside with some freshly made coffee in a travel mug to give Angel and wish her a good morning. Also, to see if Angel might have any last-minute questions.

"Mornin', Officer Stel, yawl didna' need to get up to see me off."

"Had to get up anyway; have some things to take care of before I go in later for my night shift; I just thought you could use this while you have a look around the lake,"

She claims as she hands the travel mug of coffee to Angel and continues,

"Do you have any other questions for me about this case?"

"First, lets' me ah thank ya for the coffee."

"You are entirely welcome, Angel. Now, any questions?"

"Well, I did me some thinkin' last night whilst lying in bed bout what ya told ta me about those missins' persons, and was just ah wonderin' iffin you know how many and how old they are?"

"Okay, off the record, I was told there are four teenagers reported missing right now; one boy and three girls. I'm not able to tell you their names; missing persons are not in my department; I am mainly on traffic-related cases, sorry."

"What their names is don't make no never mind ta me, I'm just ah hopin' theys is still alive, is all, has me a thing bout protectin' young peoples' and childrens'."

"We all do, Angel, so, when you get finished with your daylight re-con, come on back here for lunch; we can have a Barbeque."

"Now that just ah sounds Kool Beans to me, loves me some Barbeque. Do ya makes' your own sauce?"

"I sure do, screaming hot, too!"

"I will surely be comin' back to have me some ah that!"

"Good, Angel, see you later, and as I said, I don't go on duty until later; I'll be out there tonight, so if you need any backup, here's my contact card with my cell number you just call."

Angel puts Officer Stevenses' contact card in her breast pocket, but before she starts up her Harley, she puts on her Helmet, lifting the face shield and, she inquires of Stevens,

"I do have me one more question for ya?"

"And what is that?"

"Is there a road that goes entirely round your Oneida Lake?"

"Yes, there is, and it is appropriately named the Lake Road; it tightly goes around the lake; I have driven it every night and some days as well."

"Thanks, ya for that and again for this here coffee."

"No prob, you just be vigilant out there."

"Always does!"

Angel then starts up her Harley and speeds off down the road. When she approaches the Oneida Lake road that goes around the water, she drives to the far side to get a panoramic view of the area, landscape, and Church building—observing for all the places someone may use as an escape path if they decide to take flight. Also, to find the best way for her to make an undetected approach to observe and listen to what is going on inside.

She slowly drives around the side of the Lake where this Church is standing, leaving her Harley about thirty yards away in among some trees to have it hidden from the road; she dismounts and walks casually down the road and up to the building, taking notice of one set of tire tracks and that no one seems to be around, so then walks to the back of the building to find only one boarded up window at the first level with oddly shaped wooden planks making slits for her to be able to see in without entering the Church, for now.

In the daylight, she gets a really good layout of the inside. She observes double front entry doors that look to her not to have any heavy locking device, which opens to a single middle aisle. But oddly, she also observes no back or side doors; the only entrance or exit is the front doors. It is what appears to her the inside of a typical Church, although stripped of anything to do with any God that she is acquainted with; of course, there are two rows of wooden pews separated by the single middle aisle and at the front, an elevated dais with a center podium, but strangely there is a sizeable wooden table behind it, where a Holy Altar of some kind would be, this table is set in an angled up position. She takes note that this table, from what she can see of it from the back, looks to have leather straps at the edge of each corner, and in front of all that, an open area where it appears people would stand to listen to whoever is speaking, giving a sermon of some nature, she thinks,

Strange, this is not the usual set up for Church services; someone or someones is ah holdin some kind of ceremony here, but ta me, it ah lookins' like an Evil one, I do reckon these just ah might be ah Satan Cult. Iffin, that is the case, and I'm ah thinkin' they is. These here is very dangerous peoples. And I knows just how I's can handle em. I's hads' come up again these same types down South.

Her train of thought is interrupted when suddenly she hears a vehicle drive up to the Church's front and stop. Still looking inside, the front doors open, a formidable-looking rather tall, dark man in a black hooded cloak, carrying a black book, he is what seems to be to her to be the leader, walks-in with the group following him; now she gets a look at just about how many of them there are. With them seemingly now all inside, she carefully makes her way around the building, ducking under any of the side windows, so as not to be seen, therefore unnoticed by anyone inside, she makes her way to the front of the Church, where she sees currently parked, just where the earlier observed tire marks are; an old white Volkswagen Van, which looks to be from the nineteen sixties. Walking by it, she takes a quick look inside the Van to see nothing of any consequence, so she gets to the road to walk back to where she had left her Harley hidden off the road in a densely wooded area.

Now sitting on her Bike, she has some thoughts,

With it being a bright sunny day and noticing that they seemed to be ah havin' not any trouble with it,

She ruminates conclusively,

They just ah can't be Vampires; unlessin'…

Leaving her thoughts right there, she puts on her Helmet, starts up the Bike, pulls out, and up onto the road to head back to Officers Stevenses' place for the aforementioned Barbeque.

After having Officer Stella's delicious Pork Ribs, they sit back to relax and enjoy some of Stella's homemade Lemonaid.

"So Angel, how did your re-con go? You get all you needed for what you will do to get them, people, out of here?"

"Yup, I believes I does, do believes I does have all I needs'!"

"Good, as I said, if you need me, just call."

"Iffin, I do; I certainly will!"

"So, about what time will you be heading over there?"

"Just as soon as its ah startin' to get dark, I'll ah be on ma way. And Stel I do has me a better understandin' of why your Captin' call the U.S. Marshals for our help."

"Might I ask, how's that?"

"There are youngins' involved, an ya just can be ah raidin' ah place with them in there could be gettins' em killed!"

"And Angel, we don't want that now, do we?"

"Nope, we sure as heck don't!"

"I will be ah calling when I be ah needins yous to come to get these here people and take em into Police custody."

"Now that will be awesome! I will be looking forward to that happening! But, believe you me; this whole town will be happy to see them gone, whatever they are, and what on earth they have been doing out there at our beautiful Lake Oneida!"

"And Stella, after I takes' care ah these peoples, and this here incident be ah overa,' I'd be ah suggestin' to yawl, ta tear down that there old Church, it's an eyesore and ah dangerous place for anyones' to be inside of."

"Believe me, Marshal, I been saying that for some time now; Angel, like some more Lemonade?"

"Why sure, ya makes it just likes' we does down in Louisiana!"

"My mom's mother was from there. It's her old recipe."

"Sure can be ah small world, I reckons'."

Officer Stella Stevens agrees by humorously declaring,

"I'd says', ya do reckons' that to be ah right!"

And with that said, they both have themselves a good laugh.

THIRTY-ONE

Victor Sits Up in bed, re-reading the novella 'Mystic Vampyres' written by Rachael Valli, authored in her pen name Mia Harkness, which also had been her alias identity.

Seated at the Desk, in their room, Rachael requests of Victor.

"Victor?"

He places a Bookmark on the page he was reading from, lowers the Book, and looks over to her; responding,

"Yes, my dear?"

"How would you feel about us taking a little road trip?"

"Where to; my love?"

"I've been searching online for things and places we could do and a few places we might like to go to."

"Such as?"

"Well, let me see here, you being from the South, I'm pretty sure you do like barbequed Ribs. Right?"

Victor gets out of the bed, stands, and humorously reacts,

"So, are you now stereotyping people from the South, commenting on what they like to eat?"

"Well, like I once said to my mom, if the Shoe fits!"

"Shoe…?" Victor looks around on the floor and playfully demands,

"Shoe? What Shoe? I thought I heard you say Ribs!"

"Funny, my mom reacted the same way to that cliché statement!"

They both laugh. When their laughter dwindles, Victor moves to behind Rachael, sitting at her Laptop.

"Okay, you have aroused my curiosity, so show me what you have found."

He leads in to get a closer look at the screen, showing the web page with a map, to and for 'Billy Joe's Rib Works' restaurant up in the Town of Newburgh, New York.

"As you can see here, Victor, on this computer map, it's on the other adjacent side of the River, along the Hudson Riparian.

Racheal begins to inform him, and she continues,

"We will need to drive North on Route Eighty-Four and cross over using the Beacon Bridge on Route Fifty-Two."

Victor leads back, straightens up, smiles announcing,

"Oh yeah, that's ah lookins' real good, ta ah good ol' Southern boy like me! Yup, woulds' just love me; some of them there, Ribs! Sure wishin' we had us a Harley for this here trip! so when do we go?"

Rachael begins to giggle, saying,

"Wait, a tic! Has your Southern accent come back all of a sudden, or are you…?

"Yup, I'm just playing with you, babe; Valice would never let me speak that way at any time or all the time!"

"Oh, okay, I thought so, and by the way, have you given any thought of a Surname for Valice yet. And has Valice been in contact with you lately, Victor?"

"He was when I went out to get a Blood feeding from a Deer several nights ago. Other than that, I have not heard from, Valice. And no, I have not thought about a Surname yet. Does Valice really need one, my love?"

"Yes, we should stop calling it, only Valice. So, we can take our road trip tomorrow. If you like?"

"Yup, I would like that very much! We can discuss a Surname for, you know who, on our day trip."

"Good, then tomorrow we shall go."

"I'll tell Mike we are taking ourselves a day trip to Albany to tour the Capital City of New York State and will be gone for most of the day. We should return later that evening."

"Why tell him, or tell anyone where we will be going, even if it's not our true destination?"

"Well, my love, it's just to be respectful to others that may or may not care about us, is all."

"That does make good sense in a way, I guess."

"Victor, sweetheart, it makes perfect sense."

"In the meantime, Rach, I am heading up to that 'Horseman Tavern' tonight to see if I can find and get me and Valice our first time together Human Blood Passion feeding, and don't you worry, dear, I do remember all you told me about finding someone that is just passing through on business and how to go about executing it and also covering my tracks."

"Good, my love, you just be extra careful that no one sees you do any of it, and also please to remember, never ever give a last name, just use your short name of Vic, plus never say where you are living or staying!"

"Yup, I'll remember; I'll go there tonight right after we have our dinner. Maybe, while I'm gone, you could start doing some more writing or at least give it some serious thought."

"We can talk about that at dinner."

"Yup, okay, by the way, Jeannies' Tomato Soup is fantastic!"

"I know, had a lot of it when I was living here under my alias of Mia Harkness, writing the Book. Ben told me about it and would let me know when she had or was making it! It is truly great! Might be it will be on tonight's menu."

"That would be nice, and speaking of your Book, I'm going back to finishing my second reading, and by then, we can go down for dinner."

"I'll just grab myself a shower."

Victor, now back in bed laying upright, picks up the Book, opens it from where the Bookmark is, and merely replies,

"Mmmm."

At dinner, they speak softly to one another as they enjoy Jeannie's delicious Tomato Soup, happy to find that it's on the menu this evening. Benjamin, working as the water server, tops off their water glasses. He pardons himself to ask of Rachael,

"Any word, Rachael, from your cousin, Mia, about her writing another book about the 'Mystic Vampyres'? What she did write was very cool but short; I was hoping for more story."

"So sorry, Ben, she has not said anything about it to me as of yet, but one can only hope."

"Well, I'm hoping for more! You will let me know if she decides to do some more on it, please?"

"I sure will, my boy!"

"Thanks, enjoy your dinners, bye."

"Thank you, Ben. I've no doubt that we will!"

"See there, her number one fan wants more from yo… I mean your cousin Mia."

"Yup, Victor, I gathered that; I will give it some serious thought while you go do what is needed for you to do."

With their dinners finished, they head to their room for Victor to freshen up before heading to the 'Horseman Tavern' to hopefully acquire a victim for his very first Human Blood feeding, which shall complete his transformation so that his alter ego Valice, once known to Michael Valli as Malice and to Marlena Varlino as Menace; will be constantly aware and born a-new in Victors' mind and body. Only then can Victor understand his full potential of his new life as a Living Human Vampire.

As he walks to the Tavern, he does not feel nervous at all, just figuring that Valice from within his deep subconscious is giving him confidence and strength; Rachael's advice also is a great help to him; as Victor walks along, he thinks how difficult it must have been to do this without knowing how to go about it successfully, and not get caught. After all, it is the deliberate and wanton murder of a Human being. As the Tavern comes in view, he clears his mind of these thoughts, only now with the single one, that for him and Valice to thrive and survive, this deed, no matter how sinister, must be achieved. He takes in a deep breath and slowly enters the Tavern. Right away, he notices a woman sitting alone at the Bar and thinks,

Ah, potential.

The only seat at the Bar open to him is the one right beside her, for the place is quite full of patrons engrossed in watching a frantic sports event; as he takes the empty seat, she looks over at him, he announces loudly, to be heard over the cheering,

"Good evening, I'm Vic. And you are?"

"Not here for the sports event on the Television."

"Well, I meant your name, but I understand that the level of noise is hindering any conversation we may try to have. Shall we step outside to continue?"

She finishes her drink places some money on the Bar; Victor quickly picks up her money and hands it back to her, gestures to the Bartender to come to him. Joe the Bartender comes to him somewhat distracted by the sports event; Victor rises from his seat, leans in over the Bar, and inquires in Joe's ear,

"Joe, how much does the lady owe?"

Joe informs him, and he puts down the payment on the Bar, with a healthy tip, so they take their leave of the Tavern.

Now outside where the light of the full moon illuminates the night, he asks of her,

"Where are you parked?"

She replies,

"No Car, I traveled here by Train."

He thinks,

Perfect.

"So you don't live around here?"

"No, just passing through on Business."

"Business, huh? And what Business is that, um?"

She extends her hand to him and says,

"Names Monica, I am a sales representative for a somewhat well-known Ladies' fashion manufacturer in New York City. Just sent in an initial good size sale from the A B Ladies shop just down the street from here."

"When is your next Train due?"

"Oh, not for a few hours, now. Came here to celebrate the sale while I wait for it."

"Well, it's such a nice night. You up for a walk by the River?"

"Why not? I certainly have the time, and you seem nice enough."

As they walk along the Hudson River Bank together, she tells him all about her job; he acts very interested in what she has to say. He takes over the conversation by telling her how attractive he finds her to be as they stop in a small clearing. She stops at a tree where she seductively turns round to be face to face with him; he leans down to her as to caress her neck with a kiss, and as he does this, unseen by her, his eyes turn red, along with his fangs extending.

He holds on to her tightly and quickly endeavors to sink his long sharp fangs into her neck, rapidly sucking out enough of her Blood so as she, without a sound, passes out, her body going limp in his arms; he can now take it all in; the effect is somewhat overwhelming for him, so much so, that he drops to his knees, taking her now unconscious body with him. While on the ground, he finishes her off, her body now completely lifeless. Suddenly, he rears up as a wolf would do, to bay at a full moon, letting out an ungodly howl.

Gruffly he hears piercingly in his mind,

It is done, well done. We can now be conjoined as one!'

So now, with a sardonic smile and a profound feeling of satisfaction as instructed, they, Victor and Valice, stand up to thoroughly cover their tracks, sure to clear their clothing of any debris. And slowly, but ever so boldly, head back to the Inn, where his beloved Rachael is waiting for his triumphant return to her.

THIRTY-TWO

Rachael Sits At the Desk in front of her closed Laptop, with her right hand on the top of it holding her glass of Wine; her left hand impatiently drums her fingernails on the Desk, earnestly trying to relax and enjoy some of her favorite Vino.

While anxiously awaiting Victors' anticipated return to the Inn. She had been giving some thoughts about continuing the 'Mystic Vampyers' story with a second Book; from the initial Book that she started writing in her hometown of Mystic, and then finishing it in Sleepy Hollow in her alias identity and pen name of Mia Harkness; that she had created for her when she felt that the Mystic authorities were coming; 'to close for comfort,' and finding out the truth about her having been born a Living Human Vampire Lovechild, inherited solely from her father. Also, she was starting to believe that her mother was going to sell her out to them. Her first Book, 'Mystic Vampyres,' a Vampire love story Novella, which is very loosely based on her real father, a Living Human Vampire, and her mother a normal Human; was then published while living here at the Riverside Bed and Breakfast in Sleepy Hollow, New York State.

Victor enters the Lobby of the Riverside B and B Inn. He cordially greets Mike, who is in his usual place, sitting on his elevated chair behind the reception counter, leaning forward, with his face buried in some paperwork on the counter.

"Good evening, Mike."

Mike stops writing, lifts his head, smiles, and politely replies,

"Well, for me, it could be, if not for this constant paperwork; hope you're having a better evening than I am, Victor? Is there anything I can do for you, anything at all?"

"No no, Sir, so very sorry I didn't mean to disrupt you working there on your stuff, but yes, Mike, I have had a good one so far; I must say it has been, and I could add, just about perfect."

"That's okay; Victor can't really talk right now anyway; do need to go into the Kitchen to ask my sister Jeannie something I just found in the accounts; you have yourself a good rest of your evening."

"I shall try, thanks."

He replies as he slowly makes his start up the stairs to his room, thinking,

Oh yes, Mike, some rest is precisely what I need right about now.

Rachael opens their room door, adjusting it to stay open, then steps into the hallway and waits, having strong female emotional, intuitional feelings that Victor will show up soon, and to her relief, her instincts are precise, he sluggishly tops the stairs as she is standing in the hallway just outside the open door to their room, pleased to see him. She rushes to him, as he continues to stagger toward her, just barely making it, as he collapses into her arms; with no one else in the hallway, she brings out her Vampire powers of strength to be easily able to help him into the room then to their bed, where Victor tells her a sketchy version of how it when before he falls off to sleep. She gives him an affectionate kiss on his lips then sweetly says,

"Sleep, my darling, sleep; I will be right here for you when you awaken."

Angel believes it is dark enough now; to go to the abandoned Church and do what she has been sent here for; after checking and loading her Semi-Automatic Shotgun, then secures it back to the

fork of her Harley, she similarly makes a check of her other Weapons to see all are ready and in good working order.

Likewise, she looks at her Cellphone to be assured that it is fully charged, remembering she has set the key number nine for a speed dial call to Officer Stella Stevens, who will be out there on her own nightly patrol duty. Feeling now all is in readiness, she adorns herself with her full-face customized Helmet, starts up the Bike to head out to yet another one of her extraordinarily Earthly assignments.

She drives the long way round the Lake. So as not to pass in front of the Church. Comes round on the dark and thickly wooded area on the far side of this very old abandoned building, away from any line of sight from any of the windows, stopping not too close by, shuts off the engine, dismounts the Bike, leaving her Helmet on, slowly and very quietly walks her Bike up closer to the Church, removes the Shotgun from the fork, and what other Weapons from one of the two Saddlebags that straddle the back wheel, she believes may be needed. As she carefully walks past the Church's front to make her way to the back of the building, she can see flickering flame light coming from within, through all the windows; she can also faintly hear muffled voices that are coming from inside. She quietly makes her way to the single back roughly boarded-up window and just watches through the odd spaces between the nailed-up planks for a while to take in where people are positioned and listen for a time.

Seen from the back a seemingly large male, apparently, their leader, cloaked in a shiny black hooded robe, recites aloud while standing at a central podium reading audibly in Latin from an open book, with a group of about nine or so people, dressed in the same fashion, gathered together standing in front of him, responding to him by repeating what he has just read to them. Hearing his words, she understands most of them and thinks,

I do kinda' believes that I recognize that there Book he's ah readin' from, but my God, where could he have gotten it? Iffin it is the one I think that it could be; it's one of them there extremely rare and dangerous literary workins' from a longs time ago; I needs to hear me a little more

just to be ah sure iffin it is an authentic one of them three still existin' copies.

She continues to watch and listen, who she now with certainty believes this person is their leader, as he motions with a strange-looking large knife to two of his followers to come over to him; he speaks softly to them, saying something that she can not hear, he points to one of the young girls. Then points to the angled up table; they move quickly to grab her, bringing her over to the table to secure her to it with the leather straps, and as they gag her, he goes back to reading from the Book, and his following statement is,

"And in conclusion, Door Nine conveys to us, my truly devoted believers;

I know Now that from the Darkness comes the Light."

That statement triggers an old memory for her of this Book in question, and it is now time for her to end these proceedings.

She then takes three long strides back from the window and brings up the Shotgun and fires, quickly blowing a large opening in the old rotted wood wall. Swiftly she steps through before any of them can make a move; needless to say, they are all considerably stunned by her actions, she authoritatively announces, loudly,

"Everyone freeze! In the name of the U.S. Marshals' Department. Yawl, are under arrest!"

One person makes a start for the front doors, so she fires up at the ceiling, and that person stops in their tracks, then she repeats,

"I says freeze! And yawl of ya gets on ya knees and puts your hands behind your head!"

They do not move. And she adds, loudly,

"NOW!"

They all immediately oblige her. Except for the large man at the podium, he stands very still, just clutching the Book to his chest and his knife down by his side. At this point, she takes out her Cellphone, taps the nine key, and says, "Okay, come on, I got 'em all."

She hangs up and puts the phone in her pocket, then orders two of them to release the girl on the table; they do as she says, and then they go back to kneeling on the floor. As she waits for the Bridgeport night shift Police Officers to arrive, she approaches the man with the Book and asks of him, as she yanks it from his grasp to examine it to be sure,

"Wherever did you get yaself a copy of this here Book; The Nine Doors to the Domain of Darkness'?"

He gives her an explanation of how he came to have possession of the Book,

"A woman in New York City was selling, on the sidewalk, a table full of what looked to be primarily a man's belongings. She said it was her roommate Marc's effects and that he had gone to visit with his mom up North in his hometown of Mystic, Connecticut, and he didn't come back; she was told that he had drowned in a boating accident. She had been advised by his mother to sell his stuff to help her pay the rent; the Book was among them, so I bought it; I do believe she had no idea of what she had in this Book, so I was able to buy it; rather cheaply."

"Yup, but you'd be ah knowins' what it was, I'd ah reckon?"

"Oh yes, did I ever!"

At that very moment, a number of the Bridgeport Police vehicles, one being a large Van, pull up outside; several Officers enter the Church bursting through the front doors, brandishing their Weapons, and begin to escort the group of people out and into the large Police Van. Angel holds her Shotgun against the chest of this leader of the group, ordering him to drop the knife that he is now holding behind his back; it falls to the floor with a loud clang, as Officer Stella approaches and asks,

"Marshal, Is this person their leader?"

"It sure is, and iffin I was you, I'd put him in handcuffs afor ya be ah takein' em out of here."

Stella goes around behind him and applies her handcuffs to his wrists, picks up the knife off the floor, then leads him outside, placing him into the back of one of the squad cars.

Angel looks around to see that no one is left inside; she notices a large bunch of burning candles on a large circular pedestal table. Hip aiming at this structure, she fires at it, making all the candles go flying off in different directions, setting the old Church building ablaze; she slowly backs her way out through the now wide open front doors, thinking,

Burn, baby, burn.

With the 'Nine Doors' Book under one arm and her Shotgun under the other, she makes her way to where she had left her Harley. Puts the Book in one of the Saddlebags; just as Officer Stella pulls up on her Police Harley shuts it off and comments,

"Hey Marshal, you sure did make quick work of them."

"Well, yup, Stella, it's ah what I do best. What I'm here for and am ah real good at, an mostly the main thin' is no ones' got hurt, so iffin I'd was you, I'd just let that there old useless building burn to the ground. And be ah done with it."

Officer Stella looks over at the burning building and has an agreeable reply,

"I'm sure not going to call in the Fire Department at this hour; see ya back at the house."

Stella then starts up her Bike and drives off.

Angel secures her Weapons, mounts the Bike, starts it up, turns the Bike for her to be facing the now burning Church that is now engulfed in flames, smiles with satisfaction inside her shaded face shield, which shows a reflection of the burning Church; throttles up making her way to Officer Stella Stevens' place for a good night's sleep.

As she rides, she is deep in her thoughts of,

So I'll reckon tomorrow after I makes my report for the Bridgeport Police and the DC Marshals' Office, I'll be ah fixin' to be headin' South for the Riverside Bed and Breakfast in that there lovely little Town of Sleepy Hollow to find out, iffin that there, gall dang Author Harkness is there and is still alive. Also, that dank 'Nine Doors' Book; do has a life of its own. I'd have'ta reckon, that I'll be a needins' to do somethins' with it, right quick, afor it falls into the wrong hands. Just can't be ah lettin' that happen, never ever again.

THIRTY-THREE

Rachael Gives Some thought to how she could or would continue the 'Mystic Vampyres' story; while she has a glass of Wine, waiting for Victor to wake. Victor begins to stir; she hears the bed squeak as he slightly thrashes about; he suddenly stops, now lying on his back, turns his head in Rachaels' direction, his red eyes wide open, as he lets out one word,

"Vigorous!"

Rachael questions,

"Vigorous?"

Victor unsteadily rises from the bed to sit on the edge, lowers his head running his hands through his hair, takes in a deep breath, and slowly now stands. Rachael sees that he may need her help, so she quickly rises from her chair to go to his aid. He puts up his hand to her in a stop motion. She freezes, sitting back down at the Desk. He questions her,

"Did I say something?"

"Yes, one word."

"One word. What word?"

She replies,

"Vigorous!"

He begins to questioningly repeat the word…

She stops him and implies,

"Vigorous; a Surname for Valice, perhaps?"

"Maybe, could be, let's see how it sounds,

Valice Vigorous. So my love, what do you think?"

"Well, you hear anything from him?"

"No more than a soft, slightly agreeable murmur."

"Okay, then Victor, that is done. What time would you like us to get going on our little road trip? You still do feel up for it?"

He sits back down on the bed, answering her,

"Yes, I feel just fine, full of energy; come here, and I'll show you just how up I feel."

Angel sits at Officer Stella Stevens' Kitchen table, enjoying a cup of morning coffee. Stella exits the Bathroom into the Kitchen, pours herself a cup, and sits.

"So what now, Angel?"

"Well, I needs to make a report for your Boss and mines Boss, Director Hughes of the U.S. Marshals Department. So iffin' yous has a Computer, I can use it to get it done here, or we goes to your Police Station and does it there."

"I have one; give me a moment, and I'll get my Laptop for yeah."

Stella returns with her Laptop, places it down in front of Angel, opens it, sits down next to her, and says,

"Okay, there you go!"

Angel logs in with her password into the secure U.S. Marshal agent's website to be able to bring up a blank report to be filled in.

Stella suggests,

"Why don't I make us some breakfast, then you can dictate it to me, I would just love to hear the details, and I'll type it in for you?"

"That sounds ah might grand ta me!"

After a delicious Breakfast, Stella fills in the blanks on the page and turns to Angel and anxiously states,

"Ready for the account of how it all went down."

Angel dictates; the how and why details of the ordeal, and when she finishes, Stella sits back in her chair and amazingly remarks,

"Wow! You are good and seem to know what you are doing; I sure wish you could stay around a while and give me some of that training."

"Well, yawl sends that off to where it ah needs to be ah goin', the U.S. Marshals location is right there on the bottom of the page, and yawl' can sents' it over to your Captin' too. Sure do wish I could stay round these here parts, but I've places to go and some peoples to see."

Angel gathers up her things and heads outside to her Bike, where she stows her stuff in the Saddlebags, secures all, and shakes Stella's hand; Stella pulls her in closer for a friendly hug.

With no more words, Angel mounts her Harley, puts on her Helmet, starts the Bike, then heads off South to Sleepy Hollow.

After a light Breakfast, Rachael and Victor stop in the lobby at the Check-in Counter to inform Mike of them being out for the day. He wishes them a safe and fun day trip to their location. Thanking him, they leave to head North to their agreed-upon destination; as they travel on the highway, they come to a place in the road where it splits having a patch of thickly wooded area dividing the North and South roadways, curiously as they travel on their side going North, Angel traverses the highway on the other side heading South.

Rachael and Victor are seated at the Billy Joe's Rib Works restaurant, and they begin to view the menu. Rachael lowers her's and remarks,

"Victor, my love."

He lowers his menu to answer her.

"Yes, Rachael, what is it, dear."

"Well, I just wanted to ask you, has Valice made any more mental contact with you since your first Human Blood feeding?"

"Just in a dream-like state where I heard him say the word Vigorous, and then sort of agreed when we made it, its Surname. Why, is there something you want from Valice, my love?"

She lowers her head and softly says,

"Um, sort of, yes."

"Sort of what, sweetie. Why so mysterious? Just say want it is you want."

"I'm just a little inquisitive if there is any of my father's mental essence left in Valice when he referred to him as Malice, is all?"

Victor puts his hand gently on her shoulder and answers,

"Fret not, my love; I will certainly let you know if and when there is, if any."

Just then, their wait-person approaches their table to ask,

"Excuse me, please. Are you ready to order?"

Victor answers him with,

"We would like two glasses of Red Wine for now, please."

"Yes, of course, coming right up!"

Angel pulls into the Riverside Bed and Breakfast Inn parking lot, parks, and dismounts her Harley Davidson Motorcycle. She walks to the side entrance with her Helmet under her arm. Opens the door, and a small bell rings, and Benjamin stands up from the lobby bench, turns to see who it is, and becomes incredibly excited to see Angel has returned; he says out loud,

"This is so excellent! Mike, she's come back to us!"

"I can see that Ben, calm yourself, please. Angel, my dear, welcome back to the Inn. What may we do for you?"

Ben chimes in,

"Yeah, what do you want? Just say it, and we...

Mike cuts him off,

"Ben, please sit down and calm yourself; so sorry, Angel, he's just overly thrilled to see you back here."

"I ah reckoned he'd ah be!"

"Well, you reckoned right, alright. Now, what is it we can do for you, my dear?"

"Well, once again, I was ah passing through your lovely town a Sleepy Hollow and was just ah ponderin' iffin' yous just might be ah havin' me one of yawl rooms, for the night."

"Oh well, Angel, I am so sorry, but we are all booked up for the season; still, there just might be a room somewhere else nearby. Let me make a call and see."

Mike takes out his business phone book from under the counter and flips it to a page, stops at one, and says,

"Ah yes, here it is!"

"What is it yous ah got there, Mike?"

"Well, Angel, my dear, there is a relatively new Inn in the area, recently opened up by an old friend James Philips. Relax while I find out; he just might have a room for you; let me call him and see."

"Okay, Mike, I'ds be much obliged to ya for that!"

"Ben, seat Angel in the Dining room, and we'll get you some lunch while I do this."

While Angel is having her lunch. Mike comes to her sits down at the table to inform her; as he hands her a note containing the name and address of the Inn,

"Angel, he does have a room available for you, and he's holding it for you; here's the name and address."

"Thanks, ya so much; I really does appreciate this."

"It's really no problem. But might I ask, what you are doing back around here, you on one of your assignments again?"

"You ah could says' that, yes, and gots' me some personal business of ma' owns' too."

"Like, what personal business, if I could be so bold?"

"Well, yawl just mights' be able to be of some help ta me."

"So, how can we be of help?"

"Is that there Author Mia Harkness ah livins' here?"

Mike leans back in his chair and thinks,

Just what in the world is it that she might be wanting with Mia Harkness?

THIRTY-FOUR

Angel Sits Anxiously awaiting Mike's answer to her burning inquiry. Ben standing off to the side, somewhat behind Angel, has heard the question; Mike looks to him for a sign of what he should say, Ben being leary of what she may want of Mia, just nods his head in the negative. Mike is now torn between; the truth or a lie for an answer to her question. With his head down and not answering her, Angel is getting impatient and asks,

"Well, Mike, is she ah livin' here or ain't she ah livin' here?"

Just as he lifts his head to answer her, Jeannie quickly opens and appears at the Kitchen swinging door and calls out irately to him,

"Mike, I need you in here in the Kitchen right away, please!"

He answers her with,

"Yes, I'm coming, sis."

Then stands, looking down at Angel announcing,

"You go on having your lunch. I'll get back to you as soon as I can."

Unseen and unnoticed by Mike or Angel, Ben had quickly made his way into the Kitchen to tell Jeannie to call for Mike to the Kitchen so he could talk to him away from Angel. Mike enters the Kitchen and inquires,

"Jeannie, what is it you want or need of me that is so vital that it could not wait?"

"Mike, it's not me that wants you; it's Benjamin that needs to speak with you!"

"Well, okay, where is he? Ben, I'm here; what is it you want to say to me?"

Ben comes slowly out from the cooking area and approaches Mike to ask,

"What are you going to tell Angel about Mia?"

"Ben, I am going to tell her the truth, that she is not here and that…"

"No! Mike, please do not say anything about her cousin Rachael is here in her place, and especially that she has a person staying here with her."

"Why not tell her that, Ben?"

"I don't really know, but I just have a strange feeling that you shouldn't tell her about Rachael and her friend being here, is all."

Jeannie quickly chimes in,

"For land sakes, Mike, just do as the kid asks of you!"

"Okay, alright, okay, seeing that you two are ganging up on me, I don't believe I have a choice; I won't say anything about Rachael and Victor being here in Mia's stead. I'll just say that Mia is not here. Is that okay with you two?"

They both answer him with an agreeable nod.

Mike makes his way back to Angel and sits down. She inquires,

"Is everything okay in the Kitchen?"

"Yup, there was a minor problem with a faucet, so I fixed it for her, no biggy."

"Well, bout my askin' iffin Mia Harkness is here. Is she or ain't she, Mike?"

He lowers his head and says to her,

"Um, no, Angel, she is not here,"

Mike stands up and continues stating, as he pushes in the chair that he was sitting in,

"You finish up your lunch now while I get you the address of the place you will be staying at."

Having finished her lunch, Angel enters the lobby to find Mike at the counter writing out the information for her.

He raises his head to her and hands her the note, saying,

"Here you go, my dear, and your lunch is on us. So sorry we could not accommodate you."

Ben chimes in from behind her with,

"No one is more sorry than me! Still, maybe next time you're around here, you will stay with us?"

"Yup, that is just what I'm sapposin' I would be ah doin' next time I'm up here in these here parts. Woulds be real nice for me ta look forward to it, fir sure."

"Good, you have a good time while you're here, and you should visit the 'Horseman Tavern'; it's very close by to the place you are staying at."

"Thanks ya, Ben, I'll be ah checkin' it out maybe, this here night."

They both say their goodbyes to her; as she's walking to and out the side door of the Inn lobby to the parking lot, she stops and turns to them for a second, giving them both a warm smile.

Angel pulls her Harley Davidson Motorcycle out into the street from the Inn's parking lot, heading off in the opposite direction of Rachael and Victor, arriving a minute later from the other way to enter the Riverside Bed and Breakfast Inn, parking lot. Once again just missing each other.

Back in the Inn lobby at his check-in counter Mike inquires of Ben, now seated on the lobby bench, looking rather gloomy,

"So, Ben, my boy, should I be telling Rachael and Victor that Angel stopped in looking to see if Mia is living here?"

Ben raising his head slowly, answering him,

"Well, seeing that you asked for my opinion, I don't see any real need for it."

"And my sister, Jeannie, would most lightly agree with you."

"Probably she would, yup!"

"Oh, Ben, go into the Kitchen and see if she needs you for anything."

"Will do."

As Ben leaves the lobby, Mike starts to go about his business, shrugging his shoulders and shaking his head in wonderment.

Under his breath, he questioningly mutters,

"I don't know; I just don't. Oh well."

Then he goes about his days' work.

The side door chime sounds, and he looks up to see Rachael and Victor enter the lobby, hand in hand.

THIRTY-FIVE

Victor Sits Alone at a table away from the bar of the 'Horseman Tavern,' just relaxing sipping a glass of Red Wine.

At the bar, a good-sized group of energetic and somewhat loud patrons are engaged in viewing an enthusiastic sporting event on the large Television up on the wall at the far end of the bar, in which he is not slightly interested in viewing at all. His location is in a dimly lit corner of the place away from the bar, although he is in sight of the two entry doors, watching for Rachael to arrive.

As Rachael is leisurely walking along, making her way to the Tavern, she calls Victors' Cellphone to inform him of her coming; he, in turn, tells her where he is seated in the Tavern. She requests of him to order her a glass of Red Wine. He concurs with her request and signals to the Bartender for another glass of Red Wine. Rachael arrives and looks around, at where he said he's seated, quickly finds him sitting in the place he told her he'd be. On her approach to him, he stands, leaving his chair out, then shifts to the chair on the opposite side, putting his back to the room and the entry doors. She notes how busy the Tavern is tonight; Victor just smiles at her and drinks his Wine. She has an uneasy feeling, so she keeps an eye on the entry doors; Victor keeps turning his head to see what she is looking at or for. He leans in to speak to her, asking,

"You are keeping a steady vigil on the doors. What's up with that? Are you expecting someone from your past to show up?"

"Well, I guess you could say that; I just have an eerie feeling tonight is all, might be nothing, but it may not, I don't know."

Abruptly there is a loud uproar from the game watchers, simultaneously; the door near the Television opens as Angel steps in; Rachael sees her and says to Victor,

"Whatever you do, do not turn around. Angel just walked in; she is finding herself a seat at the bar, I don't think she can see my face from where she is, and she may not even recognize me as the person she talked to at your house when I answered the door and told her I was your house sitter while you were away on your so-called sabbatical."

"Rachael, why don't we just leave? It's too noisy in here anyway, making me very uncomfortable."

"Yes, okay, the next time there is an uproar, we can make our way to the other door from the one she came in. You go first, keeping your face away from the bar area; I will kind of hide in front of you just in case she casts a look in our direction."

The sports announcer on the Television seems to be building to a significant event, so it seems obvious there will be an uproar of the spectators coming soon, which should create the opportunity they will need to take their leave unnoticed.

Rachael can reasonably approximate what their bar tab amount should be, so they will just leave what is owed with a healthy tip on the table and make their exit.

As anticipated the team, they are mostly cheering for scores, and the place erupts with cheers, hooting, and clapping.

Rachael and Victor stand to make their exit concealed by the chaos from the sports spectators. As they make their way to the exit door with Rachael in front of Victor, which hides her from the view of the patrons and the Bartender alike, the only thing anyone can see is the back of Victor, which Angel just happens to take note of and knowing Victor as well as she does, she believes it could be him, at the worst, it would be a mistaken identity incident. So she signals to the

Bartender that she will be right back as she gets up off the barstool heading for the door that Rachael and Victor exited through.

Now looking out the open door, she is watching them walking away, so she loudly cries out,

"Victor?"

They both hear her, and without either of them turning around, Rachael says softly to Victor,

"Do not turn around; just keep walking."

Victor mutters forlornly under his breath,

"Angel."

And ever so slightly, he begins to turn his head.

Rachael takes notice and commands,

"Victor, don't!"

He snaps his head back forward; Rachael, without another word, tugs at his hand, so they pick up the pace of their stride out of the parking lot and onto the sidewalk.

Continuing to hold the exit door open, Angel cries out to him once again, still getting no reaction from him, slowly she closes the door and sadly goes back inside the Tavern, with the thought of,

I reckon it wort' him.

As they cross the street, Rachael quickly looks back to just catch Angel closing the door. Victor questions,

"Why did we run from her? I'm not one to back down from a fight, and we are two; she is only one, and I believe she was weaponless at that. I do imagine we'd have an advantage over her."

"Victor, I… I mean we, are not ready to engage with her as of yet, and besides, she always has a hidden weapon on her. she has shot me once before, and I certainly don't want to go through that again! Come on now, my love, let's get back to the Inn. We can discuss this more there."

"Yes, okay, but she must be staying somewhere close by. Wouldn't you think?"

"Yup, she must be, but she's not at the Riverside Inn; they have no vacancies right now; Mike most likely aided her in finding a place nearby."

"So, you surmise she has been to see and talk with Mike?"

"Yes, I do, and she most likely asked him if Mia Harkness was there."

"You don't think he…?"

Rachael quickly cuts him off,

"Not too sure what he may or may not have told her; I'll speak with Ben in the morning to find out, I'm pretty sure, he will tell me what Mike said to her."

"Yup, if he even heard them talking."

"Believe me, not much gets past that kid; he's like a ghost in that place, always around but unseen. Oh, he heard them talking alright; besides, he truly likes being around Angel. I do believe he still has his boyhood crush on her."

They enter the Inn lobby, hastily greeting Mike with a good evening; he reciprocates and goes about his business as they swiftly make their way up the stairs to get to their room.

THIRTY-SIX

Victor Sits On the bedside with his head down while Rachael sits at the Desk in their room.

Victor lifts his head and looks at her, asking,

"Rachael, what now?"

"Well, my love, we can't do much about it tonight, so let us get some sleep. I will speak with Benjamin in the morning to see what he knows."

In the morning, there comes a soft knocking on their door. Rachael lying in bed sees Victor just coming out of the Bathroom to answer it; she sits up in the bed, puts her hand up to him in a stop motion, and softly proclaims,

"He's right on time! I'll get it, Victor."

She gets out of bed adorns herself with her robe saying,

"That will be Ben; you go finish doing your Bathroom stuff; you can listen from there."

Rachael opens the door to find who she expected, greeting him cheerfully with,

"Morning Ben!"

Ben stands smiling, holding a tray with a small Coffee pot, two cups along with cream and sugar, announcing,

"Good morning to my two favorite guests. I have some Coffee for you two, or if you'd rather, I can go get you some Tea and a fresh-baked muffin or a scone, if you desire them."

"Oh Ben, please come in; the Coffee is just fine for now; you can put it down there on the Desk. I'd like to ask you something; please have a seat for a moment and bear with me. What I want to ask you should not take long."

"Okay, I'm all yours; ask away!"

"A person, a woman that is, came to speak with Mike recently, please, if you will reveal to me what they talked about, I'd really would appreciate it."

"Sure! You mean Angel Seraph. Right? I do believe your cousin Mia met her when they were both here a while ago."

"Yup, Ben, that's her!"

Then he goes on to tell her the whole incidental conversation and the part he had in it. When he finishes, she asks,

"So nothing was said about Victor and me now staying in my cousin Mia Harkesses' room?"

"No, not a thing was said about the two of you being here; as I told you, I made sure of that."

"Well, Ben, thank you so much for the Coffee and all; we will see you later downstairs, okay now you may leave us to get ready for the day."

Angel sits alone with the window shades drawn, making her room dimly lit at the Ichabod Crane B&B Inn, where she is, for the time being, residing in the town of Sleepy Hollow, in New York State, with many thoughts about last night's occurrence at the 'Horseman Tavern'. She begins to think aloud,

"I'll be danged iffin that weren't my Victor, I seen last night ah leavin' that Tavern, and iffin It twas Victor; then who was the woman with him? I'm ah guessin' it was Harkness, but it can't be, I shot her in the shoulder and left her alive but incapacitated for the good Lord's elements to finish her off, and iffin they did, sure enough, she should have died back there in New York Cities' Central Park."

With those spoken aloud thoughts, off in a darkened corner of her room, a shadowy figure appears and announces to her in a gentle but firm whisper,

"Angel Seraph, that is what you are calling yourself, I do believe?"

She slowly reaches for and picks up her handgun off the table beside her and asks,

"Yes, and just who might you be? Intruder!"

"I am here to inform you of the fact that you are near to haveing your agreement to be here, rescinded by the powers that be, the very same powers that granted you the right to be here in the first place because you have had thoughts and the intentions of taking a life, and most of all, you know that is not permitted. So, therefore, while being here, one of the utmost importance of his laws is, and now I quote as it was written, 'YOU SHALL NOT MURDER'. You do remember this? And the other thing going against you, we are aware that you have fallen in love with an Earthly Human and have had Cardinal Knowledge with him on several occasions."

Angel gently lays her handgun down on the table and answers the question,

"Yes, yes, I's do; been reminded recently of the Sixth Holy Commandment. But …."

Cutting her off, ever so sternly, this mysterious visitor continues with an exceedingly enraged inflection,

"But, nothing! There are no buts for the likes of us! And your southern accent is not needed when speaking with me, so you can drop it, for I know who you really are and from whence, you originally came here from, and why you wanted to come down here in the first place, and yes, it is a very noble cause, still you need to abide by his laws, that were given to man those very many years ago, like the one I just mentioned to you."

"I know, yes I do know all the Holy Commandments given to the people of the Earth. Clearly, I do, and still, I was caught up in a Human emotion after the loss of my beautiful angelic sister Gabrielle."

"It would seem to us that you were caught up in more Human emotions than just the one about poor Gabrielle. Must I remind you that Human emotions can lead to horrifying actions? That is why we usually do not have nor practice them; they can be a very destructive weakness; I do believe you have been here among them for far too long now; you are beginning to think and act as they do."

"You just may be right! Still, I feel strongly that I must finish what I have begun."

"So, is what you have started of a very critical nature to your primary mission?"

"I would say that it is. Yes!"

"I will relate to the 'Senior Ones' in upholding your request to remain a while longer, hopefully for you, they will grant you forgiveness this time, but you really must abide by the Ten Holy Commandments given to the Earthly Humans those many, many years ago, for we also are guided by them and also our granted logic, and not by Earthly Human emotions of any kind."

"I thank you, and I do wish to know who you are, or at least what you are known by, if I could."

"The appellation I was bestowed with will not be familiar to you; just let me say that I am the one that was sent to intervene in righting your wrongdoing that night in the City of New Yorks', Central Park.

Be well, and please remember you are a 'Beloved One'!"

And with that said, this unearthly visitor is gone.

Angel again thinks aloud,

"Okay, so, I think I just was, as they say down here, chewed out. But, still, I just learned that Harkness is not dead, so her Publisher told me the truth, but she is not here in Sleepy Hollow, then she must still be in Europe; if Mike was not ah lyin' ta me, then she is where they said. So I do now reckon I just may have missed somethin' while away in France on that there 'Nightstalker' mission."

THIRTY-SEVEN

After Having One of Jeannie's delicious home-cooked meals for their lunch, Victor sits at the Desk in their room, consumed with deep thoughts about the way he had feelings for Angel. Rachael is pacing the floor, wringing her hands while mumbling something incoherent that Victor can not make out.

The tension in the room is so thick you could cut it with a knife. Victor breaks the silence,

"Rachael, will you please stop pacing? Please sit down and tell me what is on your mind."

"I think what is on your mind; Victor is more important at this time."

"You believe that what is on my mind is more important than what's on yours?"

"Yes, I do!"

"And might I ask what you think or believe is on my mind?"

"Oh, Victor, stop! You think I don't know that you had feelings for her."

"Yes, I'll admit I had feelings of affection toward her."

Rachael spins around and irately says, sarcastically,

"You had feelings of affection for her? I heard you proclaim your love for her in the 'Tavern On The Green' restaurant in New York

City! So don't sit there and tell me you only had affection for her. You were in love with her!"

Victor walks to her and hugs her, saying,

"Rachael, please calm yourself; that was then; things have changed dramatically in the last several months. Please be assured that it is you I love and only you, now!"

Rachael lifts her face to him, and they kiss deeply.

They gently fall into the bed together and make mad passionate, blissful love for the rest of the afternoon.

Angel decides to stay around this town of Sleepy Hollow for a while, so she calls into the Washington DC Marshal's Office to notify them that she will be unavoidably occupied with some personal family matters for a time; and will let them know when she will be available to them again. They understand and wish her and her family well.

After removing her larger weapons off her Customized Harley Davidson Motorcycle and bringing them into her room, placing them hidden in the closet, she retains a small but powerful handgun; not wearing her regular riding apparel, she is dressed only in her street clothes.

She'll head up north along the Hudson River; for an easy ride in the upper parts of New York State's open country; in the attempt to clear her mind of all that has happened and make herself ready for anything that might occur. There is quite a lot for her to ruminate about and consider.

Riding along the Hudson River, the gentle flowing of the waters gives her a comforting feeling; forlornly, she ruminates,

There are no running rivers or streams from where I originally come here from. So if I must go back, I will miss this and much more.

She stops at a small roadside restaurant to buy some lunch to go, and then she finds a nice place along the River to have her meal. One of the first questioning thoughts she has while having her lunch is,

Is this the calm afore the storm? Will I be able to finish what I had begun and what will happen to my position with the U.S. Marshals Department? Dang, that's far too many questions right now; I'm ah guessin' I'll just have ta wait and see how it all plays out. And also, just

who might that be that I spoke with in my room just ah wonderin' iffin I know them, is all, okay Angel that's enough thinking fir now, just gonna lay back and rest afore I go on with my ride.

She closes her eyes, lays down on her back, quickly falling off to sleep on the blanket she had brought with her in one of her Saddlebags on the Bike and spread out on the ground for her little picnic lunch. After about an hour, she is abruptly awakened by the sound of someone's footsteps coming through the trees to her location, on the river bank. In her supine position, her hand moves to her gun, and she opens her eyes, sits up to find it to be, by his uniform, a Motorcycle Officer of the local town Police; she removes her hand away from the weapon, as this Officer questions her,

"Excuse me, Miss, are you alright, and is that your Motorcycle parked out there on the shoulder of the road?"

"Yup, it sure is, Officer. Ain't she a bute? Cost me plenty! Might there be ah somethin' wrong with where it's ah parked? Causen', iffin there is I can be ah movin' it right quick iffin it is, Sir."

"Oh no, it's legal where it is parked where it is. And yes, your Bike is a beautiful custom-built one, at that. It's just that other drivers going by are slowing down to have a look at it. And that's causing a back up on the road."

As she quickly gets herself up, she says,

"I'll be ah movin' it right quick for ya; I was just about done here anyhow."

Swiftly she gathers up her debris along with her Bike Helmet and things and heads out to the road where her Harley is parked. With this Officer following close behind.

At her Bike now, she places her stuff in one of the Saddlebags, mounts her Bike, but before she can put on her Helmet, the Officer stops her by asking,

"By the way, Miss, I would chance to believe that you do have a license for the Bike and that handgun on your hip? And with all due respect, may I ask, your accent, where are you from?"

She answers him while getting her driver's license and Special Agent U.S. Marshal's I.D. and Badge from her back pocket.

"Oh, yeah, I'm from Baton Rouge, Louisiana, Officer, up here on a Special Mission that is finished now."

The Officer takes her driver's license and I.D. and Badge from her, gives it an intense look, and as he hands them back to her, he respectably says,

"Okay, thank you, Marshal, here you go; you have yourself a real good rest of the day, now!"

As he walks away from her and mounts his Police issued Harley Davidson Motorcycle. Angel puts her credentials away, puts on her Helmet, starts her Bike, and decidedly thinks,

I reckon I'll ride a bit longer until it starts to be gettin' dark and then be headin' back ta Sleepy Hollow.

Rachael exits the Bathroom in her robe after a refreshing shower; to find Victor still is in bed. She wraps her still wet hair in a towel, sits at the Desk, and opens her Laptop. Victor rolls over to face her to ask and proclaim,

"Good shower, hun? And I must say that was some intense lovemaking, sweetheart."

"Great shower! And that intense lovemaking, as you put it, I believe may be needed if we are going to have a child soon."

"What you doing on your Laptop, Now? You going to be doing some more writing on that 'Mystic Vampyres' Book?"

"No, I am getting the contact number for the U.S. Marshal's Office in Washington DC."

"Why there? It's on my Cellphone. What are you planning to do with it?"

"I want to find out if she put in for some time off? It could tell us for how long she is planning to stay around here."

"Yup, maybe. Then what?"

"Oh, Victor, my darling, do I have to do all the thinking for us?"

"No, I think I see where you are going with this."

"I thought you'd catch on. You were just being coy, right?"

"Yup, just playing with ya is all, ma'am."

"Victor, come on, get up and take a shower so we can go for a nice walk along the Hudson River before having our dinner."

"Okay, boss lady!"

"Not funny, Vic!"

She gives him a love tap on his bum as he passes by her headed to the Bathroom.

THIRTY-EIGHT

"Hello, U.S. Marshal's department Washington DC Office. Agent Adams is speaking. How may I help you?"

"Yes, I sure do hope you can; I am trying to get in touch with your Agent Seraph. If I may? Please."

"Please hold."

"Okay, thanks."

Her phone goes to the musac hold music service.

Angel decides that it is about time; she started to make her way back to her room in Sleepy Hollow, so she pulls the Bike over to safely turn it around; in doing so, a car comes speeding by her from around the corner, sounding its horn as it almost hits her and her Bike. After completing the turnaround, she sits for a moment on the side of the roadway to collect herself, then shifts into gear throttle up and proceeds down the road. After riding for about an hour in the southbound direction, Angel begins to drive across the Bear Mountain Bridge, which spans the rapidly flowing Hudson River; as she is almost at the other side where it connects to the Bear Mountain road, a sizeable eighteen-wheeler tracker trailer truck comes at a high rate of speed down the declining mountain road and onto the Bridge headed toward her in the northbound direction, unknown to her this driver is dozing off, he veers over into the oncoming lane, just as Angel is almost finished passing by his rear wheels, she needs to swerve out of the truck's path or be run under this truck's wheels, the trucks back wheels just taps one of her saddlebags making her swerve and lose her control of the bike, sending her crashing through the short wooden guard rail, and then out off the Bridge. Falling fast now toward the rapidly flowing waters of the Hudson River, the Bike goes out from under her as she releases her grip on the handlebars, and she pushes off from the seat toward the river's bank.

Mind you, this is all happening and took place within seconds.

Her exquisite Custom made Black and Purple Harley Davidson Motorcycle plummets into the rapidly flowing Hudson River's waters while she lands on the dry, rocky ground under the Bridge, batted and bruised, she passes out.

The truck driver suddenly awakens and rights his truck into his northbound lane, and continues driving across the Bridge, taking no notice of the cycle rider's plight. Actually, no one else was on the Bridge or the road at the time to witness any of the instantaneous incident take place. Here only being a lone vagrant up in a deep darkened spot under the Bridge, which seemed to be sleeping, there was no one to call for any assistance at all. Finally, after an undetermined amount of time, Angel slowly opens her eyes. She finds that a moonless night has fallen, making it an extremely dark evening, indeed.

Suddenly a bright light appears behind her; she slowly and painfully turns herself over onto her stomach, lifts her head slightly to see what it can be, at first, thinking that it might be a vehicle's headlights bearing down on her. Her vision is somewhat blurred, and the pain she feels is getting worse to the point where she almost feels like she will blackout; it seems to her that she is spinning round and round, then suddenly she stops, and her vision clears enough to see the familiar image of Azrael, the Angel of Death, hovering in front of her. In her scattered thoughts, she thinks,

Oh no! no no no! not you. Not now, please!

Azrael slowly extends his Angelic, ethereal hand to her, and she can now rise up without any painful feelings, for her divine, ethereal image is now leaving her Earthly body, and the mortal Human pain she was feeling is no longer present to her. In her fading fast Human thoughts, she comprehends his words;

You have been judged guilty of misconducts and now must come back from whence you came; someone else will be sent to take your place to assume the noble acts you have been performing in defense of Earthly humanity, and also what you had begun, plus carry on with the, caring courageous deeds and labors you were accepting for his beloved Human race. So come, your time on this Earthly plane is over; it is time for you to rest back in the bosom of our divine Angelic family.

Seemingly what seems to be unnoticed by any Human eyes, the blinding bright white light slowly diminishes into the darkness, as Angel's Earthly vessel and all that is with it; turns to ash and is blown away by a strong gust of wind that comes through, under the Bear Mountain Bridge in upper state New York. The only thing left to be seen of any evidence of this incident is a distorted metal upright and a section of broken wooden guard rail protruding off the road, out over the water on the southbound side of the bridge roadway. Drivers now passing by pay very little mind to it but imagine that something terrible has happened here, but they can not know when it may have taken place. All is quietly serene now on and under the Bear Mountain Bridge except for the flowing waters and a vehicle or two from time to time passing over it.

Victor enters their room after having an early evening's brisk stroll along the Hudson Riverbank. Rachael has just put her Cellphone down on the Desk and now has a very unsatisfied expression on her face; so Victor inquires,

"How did you make out with your call?"

"Not good really, they only could tell me she has requested extended personal leave for a family matter, and they do not know when she will be back for service. Also, they informed me that they do not have anyone who can do her job right now. How was your walk? Victor."

"Okay, but as I stopped to watch the Hudson River's waters flowing by me, something came over me like a very intense feeling of loss and dread. I then could have sworn I saw the top of a set of

Motorcycle handlebars sticking up out of the water flow by, way out in about the middle of the river."

"Heck, Victor, that could have been some kids bicycle going down the river, and that feeling you had could have easily been indigestion from something you had eaten too fast, hun."

"Yup, it could just be; you are correct! Sweetheart. So my love, what are we up to on this fine and lovely Sleepy Hollow evening?"

THE END?

www.ingramcontent.com/pod-product-compliance
Lightning Source LLC
LaVergne TN
LVHW011941070526
838202LV00054B/4746